ENCHANTED
CASTLE
ON THE RIVER

Matt's Journey

SYLVIA ABOLIS MENNEAR

Enchanted Castle on the River
Copyright © 2021 by Sylvia Abolis Mennear

ISBN
978-1-956529-00-5 (Paperback)
978-1-954932-99-9 (eBook)

A bumpy time-traveling tale
Kirkus Indie Review

Also written by Sylvia Abolis Mennear

Shattered Dreams and Broken Hearts
'Fentanyl The Killer'

TABLE OF CONTENTS

PROLOGUE

He had been walking down the path through the woods for an hour or so when he decided to sit down beneath an withered old willow tree. It must have stood in excess of seventy feet tall, like a giant ogre with a thousand arms that hung motionlessly to the ground. This was the ideal shade tree that he truly needed to get out from under the heat of the summer's afternoon sun and rest for a while. It was a scorcher of a day, and this was the perfect spot for a rest and a snack. There were heaps of undergrowth and brushwood to make a cosy nest for him to rest in.

He had a snack, pulled his diary out of his knapsack, and wrote a few lines about the drive up and the beautiful spot that he had just found and then dozed off for a while. The summer breeze had a sweet fragrance of wild roses and lavender that gave him a soothing and yet sluggish affect. The gentle wind, with its soft spreading fingers caressing the crimson skin on his face—he could sense it blowing through his hair. It felt so tranquil that he could have spent hours with the breeze massaging his face and scalp while listening to the sounds of nature. Suddenly, he awoke to a crunching sound from behind him. He sheepishly looked over his shoulder and believed that what he saw was a small dog. At first glance, that was what he thought it was. What he wasn't aware of (there was no way he could be) was that it was a creature from a different dimension, a dimension that had been explored for hundreds of years without extensive or significant logical evidence that such a thing ever existed and only a small number of us could possibly ever believe.

The creature was small. It was not proportioned appropriately and was rather creepy looking. Whatever it was, it had powers. Powers that Matt did not understand and would take for granted throughout his unique journey.

* * * *

My name is Matt, and I'm fourteen years old. For as long as I can remember, I have been spellbound with the idea of going on a mega adventurist escape or vacation. I would dream of the day when I could choose to where I wanted to go anywhere in the world, far, far away, where I could hide from my family and friends. The only vacations that I have been on are camping with my family. That was all my parents could afford, but I don't mind. At least, my parents do what they can for us.

I have two older sisters and one younger bratty brother. My parents don't have a great deal of money. My mother cleans houses for additional money, and my dad works very hard at a dairy farm as a machinist six days a week, ten hours a day. As my parents struggled to raise four kids, we were privileged enough to go on camping trips every summer, which we all very much looked forward to.

While on our trips, I have always had a massive imagination that would take me all over the globe, and I would use that gift whenever we went camping. I liked to imagine that I was going somewhere else on the globe, out of the country, as an alternative to just camping. It made the trips truly enjoyable and adventurous.

This time, my imagination has gotten the better of me, and I'm afraid. I mean really afraid. It was fun at first, but now I don't know how to get back. At first I thought it was just a dream, but I know better now. This is a nightmare. There is just no reasonable answer as to what is happening to me.

Matt was looking at the clouds out a window of a jet plane.

There has to be an explanation. One minute, I'm sitting under an old tree, and now I'm here on a plane. Am I delusional?

Frightened, he slouched downward in his seat and dropped his face into his hands and tried to make some sense out of all of this. Then it came to him. There was one vivid thought racing through his mind: the creature that looked like a dog with the razor-sharp claws and the long snout with bulging yellow eyes, he must have something to do with all of this.

THIS IS
MATT'S JOURNEY

CHAPTER

1

It was a beautiful Saturday morning in July, in the city of Portland, Oregon. Matt's little brother, Ben, startled him out of a great sleep at 7:00 a.m., jumping on his bed and yelling "Dad said we are going camping for a few days!" all ecstatic. His brother was only six and extremely hyper. Matt really thought he had ADD.

"You jackass! Ben, get off of me! I was sleeping."

Then he started to take clothes out of Matt's dresser and tossed them on the bed. Matt yelled at him, "Hey! Stop that! I'll pick out my own clothes."

"Well, hurry up," Ben said as he ran out of the room and stuck his tongue out at Matt while slapping his butt. "Dad said we're leaving in two hours."

"Great. Saturday morning, and I can't even sleep in late."

As sleepy as he was, Matt got up and began packing for the camping trip. He loved their camping trips—except for some reason, he really wasn't in the frame of mind to go this year. He didn't know why—maybe because he was tired or maybe because he wasn't given any notice earlier than two hours. What was up with that anyways? Oh well, he might as well go with the course. Not like he was going to have a say in their plans anyways.

Mom and Dad worked hard, and they could do with a vacation, so Matt was not going to spoil it by complaining to them about how early he had to get up. So as always, prior to their departure, he set his mind to envision that he was about to embark on a trip to where he had never been before, somewhere he could only dream of going—it made the trips much more exhilarating. But he didn't have a clue where his mind would take him this year. There were so many places that he hadn't been, like everywhere and anywhere in the world, so it shouldn't be that complicated to come up with a place.

As he walked downstairs to the kitchen to make breakfast, it came to him. The movie he watched the other night, the *Life and Times of Fourteenth Century Britain*—that could be fun!

He then noticed that everyone was by now loading their gear in the Jeep. Boy, they sure were speedy. *I mean, Ben told me barely half an hour ago that we were leaving. When did Mom and Dad decide we were going camping? At five ivvn the morning?*

His mom was walking back toward the house and saw him at the kitchen window and yelled, "Hurry up and have your breakfast. We want to leave in the early hours. It's a lengthy drive to get to where we are going."

"Yeah! Can I have at least ten minutes between waking up and eating?"

So he grabbed the fruit-flavored cereal out of the cupboard and poured a bowlful, sat down, and ate his breakfast.

Ben came charging into the kitchen. "Are you ready yet, Mr. Fruit Loops? And where is your duffel bag?"

"Enough with your morning sarcasm, Ben. I want to eat my breakfast. My bag is at the front door, so if you're so anxious to do something, then put it in the jeep for me." Matt noticed that his two older sisters weren't anywhere in sight, so he asked, "Hey, Ben, how come Kim and Becky aren't here?"

Ben shouted back at Matt as he was picking up Matt's bag. "They're going on a camping trip with their friends from down the street. They left last night. So now there will be a lot more room in the jeep, and by the way, I get the window seat!" he yelled on his way out the front door.

"Well, there is simply you, me, Mom, and Dad, so I think we both get a window seat. What an airhead," Matt said as he rolled his eyes.

He grabbed the funnies that were lying across the table from him. He started to read them while he was eating his cereal. He always loved the funnies, especially *Peanuts* with Charlie Brown. He came across an ad in the paper, right across from the funnies, looking for new members to join a medieval jousting group. *Wow, that looks so cool, everyone dressed up from that era. I'd love to become a member of that,* Matt thought to himself. So he tore the article out of the paper and stuck it in his pocket. Just then, his mom and dad came back in to get some more gear and groceries.

"Are you near ready, Matt? I know we threw this at you quite sudden, but it is summer holidays, so being impulsive isn't really that extreme, is it?" His mom said with raised eyebrows.

"Where are we going this year, Mom?"

"Well, your dad was browsing through the road map last night and said that we should head north this year. Isn't that right, dear?" She motioned to his father to carry on telling Matt where they were heading to as she continued to pack up the rest of the food on the counter.

"That's right, Matt. We'll drive until we find a campground that looks appealing to all of us."

"Actually, he did find one just north of the border called the Hidden Woods. Sounds cozy, so as long as we are all in agreement when we pull into the campsite, then we'll stay there," Mom said.

"Ya, Mom, it sounds mystifying," Matt sarcastically said.

"If we leave within the hour, we should reach our destination by nightfall, taking into consideration that we will make a few stops on the way. How does that sound, Matt?" Dad asked.

As Matt ate his cereal, he managed to speak. "It sounds cool. You know I love the outdoors and the adventures. The Hidden Woods"—for a moment, he mumbled to himself—"Huh. Hmmm. Interesting name for a campsite. Do you suppose there are bears roaming about, Dad?"

"Well, Matt, I presume that the northern coast and interior have a lot of bear sightings. Remember, this is a campground, so there would be precautions for the guests. Just make sure you read all the signs posted and adhere to them!" His father said as he left the kitchen with a bag of groceries. He got about five steps away and turned around. "Oh, and, Matt, you in particular have to play it safe! Your mother and I know how your imagination can get the best of you at times. If you recall last year's escapade! If your mother and I knew you wanted to try to be a cattle herder, we could have brought you to a ranch to get an understanding of the animal. But just going off and herding cattle in addition to scattering them all over the highway? Well, that was a time in our lives where we could have locked you up for life. Do you remember how much trouble you caused?"

"Ya, Dad, I remember," upset that his father brought that incident up again. "I thought we had dropped it. What was done was done!"

"Matt, it's dropped, but I don't think we will ever forget it and all the hours we all had to waste to get those cattle back onto the owner's field. We must have had half of the guests at the campsite helping because of your stupidity."

"Okay, Dad! I get it. It was brainless. It just got out of hand. I didn't think—" He got cut off by his mother before he could finish his sentence.

"That's right. You didn't think," his mother said. "You will be a lot more cautious this year, won't you? We want to have some down time to unwind and not clean up after your escapades," his mom growled as she walked away.

"Don't worry, Mom and Dad, I know I have a drifting imagination, but I won't let it get the best of me this year. I won't inconvenience you guys at all, and I've grown up too."

Matt's parents looked back at him and smirked as he said that. They weren't dense. They knew he was somewhat altered and life with him was always a challenge.

"We'll see," his mom said as she grabbed a bag of groceries off the counter and headed to the jeep.

"Don't forget to rinse your dishes and place them in the dishwasher when you're done, Matt. The imaginary maid is on strike today. Oh, and I have one more trip to make back to the house, and you'd better be ready because I will be locking the house up. We wanted to be on our way by nine o'clock a.m., but as it looks, we will be lucky to be out of here by ten o'clock!"

"I'll be ready in five, Mom," Matt said as he jumped out of his chair.

"I guess I'd better put my dishes away or I'll hear about it in the car. I wonder if I will meet anyone interesting on this trip."

CHAPTER

2

"So, Dad, where are we going? I know you said the park was called the Hidden Woods, but where precisely is this place?" Matt asked.

"Well, Matt it's in a town called Lillooet, roughly eight hours up north. Lillooet was a child of the Gold Rush like so many Cariboo towns."

"Do you think there is still some gold in them thar hills, Dad?" Ben said.

"Oh, probably, little man. A lot of people still gold-pan in the rivers along the towns. Oh, I doubt you would find much more than a tiny nugget, but who knows? Anything is possible. All around these areas are ghost towns, railways, and old mines. You can learn a lot of history in a place like this. You kids can even gain enough knowledge on this trip to do an essay when school is back in session."

"Ya, right, like school is nowhere in my thoughts," Matt said with disgust. "I will do an essay," Ben said with delight.

"I'm just saying," his dad said. "I did some research online, and there are many things to see. For instance, Hangman's Tree. It was allegedly used as a gallows during the 1800s gold rush by a hanging judge. It is said that two thieves were hanged and buried beneath the tree, and legend has it that eight lawbreakers in all swung from the tree."

"Cool, I want to go see that!" Ben said.

"And then there is Bridge of Twenty-Three Camels. A resident of Lillooet bought twenty-three camels in 1862 from San Francisco for three hundred dollars. He shipped them to Lillooet to work in the gold rush as pack animals. They worked well for a while, but their tender feet, bad tempers, and foul smell led to a dismal failure. Oh, and it's not just the history. There are hiking trails, jet boating, fishing, golfing, and wildlife such as mountain goats, big horn sheep, cougar, and black bear that range in the mountains. There will be a lot to see and do."

"Sounds exciting, hey, kids? I doubt that we'll get bored. I'm so looking forward to this trip," Mom said.

Well, that was enough talk for Matt. He put on his headphones. He didn't think that he would actually fall asleep to his music, but he did. Matt slept for the most part of the drive—his brain probably just shut down. He dreamed on the whole drive until he heard his mother call.

"What a dream! I remember bits and pieces of it. I don't usually remember my dreams. This one I'll have to write down in my journal because it was so bizarre," Matt said.

"Well, don't keep us in suspense. What was it about?" Mom asked.

"I remember walking through the forest and coming across a strange animal that looked kind of like a dog, but it seemed to have supernatural powers. It lured me through the most lush and beautiful forest that I had ever seen. The sun was midway through the sky so that shadows were being cast through the evergreen trees. The smell of fresh pine and wildflowers was everywhere. There was a slight breeze blowing, just enough to keep the smell of pine and flowers lingering in the air. I can still smell it. The colors were extraordinary. The trees were green as green could be, and the flowers were pastel yellow, orange, and purple with white. I noticed not a thing was lifeless—not a flower, not a tree, not a dropped branch or leaf off of a tree—and there were even mushrooms. Not normal mushrooms. These ones were huge, like, as tall as Ben and in every color imaginable."

"Something always dies," Mom said, "whether it's a branch of a tree or an expired flower."

"That's what is so neat about my dream. It was like a fantasyland." Matt said. "And, Mom, you would love this place. It looked like a fantasy garden in the woods!"

Then Matt's mom yelled out, "We're here! And it only took us eight and a half hours, and that sounds like a wonderful dream, Matt."

"That was a quick eight hours. I guess I must have slept most of the way!"

Ben was laughing. He was so thrilled, and Matt hoped he would make some new friends this year instead of becoming a throbbing pain in the butt once again. Matt was constantly getting trapped taking him everywhere he went, because Ben always got his way. Well, no more!

This weekend, he was going to find something to do where Ben wouldn't be allowed to go.

"Okay," Mom said, "since it's nearly dusk, the only thing we are going to do tonight is help set up camp, get dinner ready, set the table, and collect wood for the fire. Agreed?"

Both Ben and Matt said "Agreed" together at the same time.

"Hey, guys, isn't tonight the meteor shower?" Dad said. "I think so, honey. Today is the twentieth, isn't it?"

"Lucky guys you are," Dad said. "You get to watch a meteor shower with your dinner tonight. Think of it as a ceremonial dinner for the first night of your vacation."

"Ya, a dinner and a show!" Ben said.

"Ah. Ha. You're pretty witty, Ben." Matt rolled his eyes at him.

Ben and Matt helped set the table for Mom as she got dinner ready, and Dad scrambled around the area looking for some firewood and kindling for their fire. He had a flashlight with him and was trying his best not to be a nuisance to anyone, but a few times, Matt heard him fall and swear. Matt's mom would yell out "Shush!"

They had just about finished dinner, and they were all sitting at the table, silent and worn out. No one said a word for about fifteen minutes, and without warning, Matt's dad yelled out and pointed in the direction of the sky. "Did you guys see that? That burst of light in the sky? Well, maybe it was a spark or a flare. It was something I've never seen before."

"No, I didn't see it. What do you suppose it was, Dad?" Matt asked.

"In truth, I'm not sure now or how to describe it. It was like a stretched-out shooting star, yet it was a dazzling yellow in color. Crazy as it sounds, it was in the silhouette of a dog," Dad said.

Ben asked, "What sort of dog, Dad?"

"Well, I don't know. Just a dog with a long tail. Sounds bizarre, doesn't it?"

Mom had Ben and Matt giggling when she said, "How much have you had to drink tonight, honey? Anyways, you may possibly see strange things since we are to see a meteor shower tonight."

Then all of a sudden, they saw a flash across the sky. Matt's dad was right. It was in the shape of a dog. What the heck could that be? The color was a brilliant yellow with a little green, and it truthfully looked like a dog. Matt knew he wasn't dreaming since the rest of the family saw it too.

Of course, his mom talked it down by saying that they were all exhausted and restless from the drive, and that after a good night's sleep, they would be recharged and as good as new in the morning. They all agreed and helped clean up and headed for their tents to sleep the night away.

* * * *

The next morning, Matt wanted to go on an exploration hike. He told his parents that he shouldn't take Ben with him because if he went astray, then they'd both be lost. They considered that a dumb excuse but let Matt get away with it. He knew what they were up to. If they let him go once on his own, then he would owe them, and if he knew them, they would have Ben stuck to him like glue for the next few days. Matt's parents said that Matt was the big brother and that he should be a superior model for Ben to follow from. Well, just because he got good grades didn't mean Ben was going to walk in his shoes. If Matt mentioned last year's fiasco with the cows every time they wanted Ben to tag along, they may change their minds, seeing how Ben would pick up some bad traits from him.

Now that's the way of Matt's philosophy. Ya, that was a howl. I would do it all over again if I knew there was no way that I'd get caught. If the cattle were to get out again, I'd say someone most likely copied what I did last year, and maybe it would become a custom. We'll have to call it Matacow. Kind of like matador.

Ya, I believe I have to consider that one once more if I can't find anything wiser to do, Matt thought as he chuckled to himself.

His mom yelled out to him. "I'll fix you a lunch to carry along just in case you overlook the time. This reminds me: wear your watch!"

"I broke it a couple of weeks ago, remember?" Matt said to his mom.

"Oh, darn it, I forgot. I was going to pick another one up for you. I totally forgot. Well, I'll let you use mine for today."

"Forget it, Mom!" he said in disgust. "It has a bright red wrist band. I don't want to look girly!"

"Oh, for crying out loud, Matt! No one will even notice it." "Sure they will. It's *bright red*, Mom!"

"Then wear a sweater or something with sleeves! You're not leaving here without this watch, Matt!"

"Now look, Matt," his father calmly said, "if it bothers you that much, then just put your mom's watch in your pants pocket. Problem solved."

"Dad, my shorts don't have a pocket."

"Then wear some that do, Matt! Why do you have to be so difficult all the time? You want to go on your own without your brother, and we said okay. Your mom asks you to take her watch so you can keep an eye on the time, so you complain about the color. I come up with a solution, and instead of you using your brains and saying 'I better wear something with a pocket in it' or 'I will be wearing the watch,' you have to act stubborn by saying 'I don't have any pockets!' Geez, Matt, I thought you were supposed to be smart?"

"Fine! I'll change my shorts." Matt really didn't want to take the watch because then he didn't have an excuse for why he was late. They always give him a time limit, and it was never long enough. *Darn that watch. I could always lose it. Hmmm. Naw, I couldn't do that to Mom. But then again, it is an ugly watch. Maybe then, Mom could go get a new one. I'd be doing her a favor!*

Matt went back into the tent to change his shorts. "Okay, I put on my shorts with *two* pockets in the front. Happy?"

"Not quite yet, Matt," his mom said. "Just so you don't lose the watch—you know how much I treasure this watch—I'm going to safety-pin it to your shorts pocket."

"Give me a break, Mom! I'm not Ben!"

"You may not be Ben, but you always have your own agenda, Matt. Your dad and I aren't stupid."

"I didn't say you were. I'm just saying that you guys never trust me, no matter what."

"It's not that we don't trust you, Matt. It's that we don't trust your extreme imagination and what it could do. We don't forget!" Mark, Matt's dad, said.

Then Ben started running back to the tent and yelled at his mom. "Where is Matt going? I want to come along too!" Ben stomped.

"No, we promised Matt that he could have the afternoon for himself. You can go out with him tomorrow, Ben," Sue, Matt's mom, kindly told him.

Then Ben started to have one of his fits, which actually worked out fine for Matthew, because while his mom was trying to calm Ben down, he took that opportunity to slowly exit the area.

Then his mom yelled out, "Matt, its ten o'clock a.m. right now. I want you back here by dinner, which gives you eight hours. Okay! That gives you plenty of time to have your alone time, and don't forget to grab your lunch off the picnic table."

"Darn it! I thought I'd be able to get out of here before she saw me, and then she couldn't argue with me that she gave me a curfew time. Crap," Matthew huffed to himself.

"You know, Sue," Mark said, "giving him eight hours on his own could get us into trouble again. Maybe we should have sent Ben to go with him, because you know that Ben gets tired in a few hours, especially if he has to walk. At least that would give us more assurance that they would be back on time."

"Yes, well, Mark, he is a year older, and I would hope that he has also done a lot of growing up in this past year. I'm giving him the benefit of the doubt. And I hope he doesn't let us down."

CHAPTER

3

"Wow, this is some trail. It doesn't look like many people have travelled it. There aren't any footprints or many broken branches. I wonder how far into the woods this trail actually goes? Maybe I should mark my way with something, just in case I get lost."

Matt reached for his knapsack, which contained all kinds of junk that he never cleaned out when school ended for the summer. While he was searching for something that might work well as a marker, he came across an unopened package of gum.

"This will work great. I'll just chew the gum and stick it to the wrapper and then bend it over the end of a branch on trees along the way. That will tell me which way I came."

So every hundred feet, Matt would chew some gum and then stick it to the wrapper and then on to the end of a branch that hung over the trail. Hoping that it wouldn't fall off, he squeezed it extra tight to make sure that it would stick really well.

He must have been walking the trail for an hour when he decided to sit down under an old willow tree that hovered over him like a giant monster with thousands of dangling arms. It must have stood over twenty feet tall, with branches that hung to the ground. This was the perfect shade tree that he really needed to get out of the heat for a while and rest.

"I think I'll have a snack. Let's see what Mom packed for me." He went through his knapsack. "Hmm. Tuna sandwich, banana, a couple of Dad's cookies, and a bottle of water. Well, that will last me all of fifteen minutes."

A short while later, when he finished his snack and drink, he started to feel a little dozy, so he nodded off for a while. The sweet smell of wild roses and the wildflowers in the summer's warm afternoon sun was so nice. The breeze, with its soft, spreading fingers, caressed his light pink skin on his face. He could feel it running through his hair. It felt so relaxing that he could have spent hours with the breeze massaging his face and head and listening to the *sounds of nature.*

He awoke to a crunching sound coming from behind him. He sheepishly looked over his shoulder and assumed what he saw was a small dog. At least, that's what he thought it was at first glance. What he didn't realize was that it was an animal from another dimension—a dimension that had been explored for hundreds of years. And why should he? There had never been any substantial scientific evidence or facts that we could possibly ever believe in.

It was very small and not proportioned correctly—a rather sad-looking dog. Whatever it may be, it had powers—powers that Matt did not realize until his journey was nearly at its end.

"What the heck is that?" he yelled.

It was about the size of a forty-five-pound dog with a long fuzzy tail and a stretched snout with awfully large nostrils. He could almost be cute with his grumpy-looking mouth, but his snout was too big for his face. He had shortish hair and pointed ears that stood straight up, almost like they were at attention or something. Its yellow eyes were bulging from its face, and its claws were so long and razor sharp.

"Man, do you need a manicure? I bet those could slice you up pretty good. If you are a dog, you have got to be the strangest-looking one I've ever seen."

Geez, I wonder if he is from Asia or Europe. He can't be from this part of the world. "So what the heck are you?" Matt asked the beastly looking animal as it was getting closer to him and trying to sniff him from a distance.

Matt was getting a little jumpy, not knowing if he should stand up and run or stay where he was. So he decided to go through his snack bag and toss his leftovers to this strange "dog."

"Here, try some of my tuna sandwich, and then you'll know that I'm okay." He threw a chunk of his tuna sandwich and some cookie crumbs to the animal. The animal then gradually came closer to the food that was thrown to him and sniffed it with his large snout. He began to eat the food given to him and sat down as he glared at Matt. With those large yellow eyes, the beast did a good job of intimidating Matt.

"Good stuff, isn't it? I wish I had some more, but I don't," he said while looking through his bag. "Actually, I have a piece of banana left, but I doubt you will like that."

He threw it to the animal, and with no hesitation, the animal grabbed it and chewed it up, peel and all.

"Wow! You must be hungry!"

Matt reached out his hand carefully to the animal to show him kindness, and the animal in return sniffed Matt's hand and licked it. Matt drew his arm back immediately when he saw the animal's tongue was green. He grabbed his shoulder, massaging it, thinking that he had dislocated it.

"OMG, your tongue is green! What are you?" he yelled as he was still rubbing his shoulder.

Matt was afraid and didn't know if he should jump up and run or just sit still and show no fear. He did the latter. The animal snorted at Matt, and Matt began to laugh with hesitation. Then the animal rolled around on the ground and kicked his hind legs up in the air while his ears were flapping like wings, and he lifted a few feet off the ground with a thrust, spun around in the air three times, and landed softly on the ground in front of Matt. Then he just sat there and stared at Matt.

The animal said in a loud whisper, ***"Over the bridge."*** His bright yellow eyes shot a laser-like light into Matt's eyes and mesmerized him into a sleep.

* * * *

Back at camp, Ben was still asking his parents if he could go join Matt.

"No way," Sue said. "He shouldn't be that much longer Ben. He's been gone now for an hour and a half. He said he'd only be a few hours, I'm sure when he comes back he will share his adventure with you."

A boy a few years older than Ben came over to their campsite and asked Ben if he wanted to hang out.

"Is it okay, Mom, if I hang out with—what's your name?" he looked at the boy.

"Shawn," the other boy said.

"With Shawn mom?" Ben said with excitement. "Shawn, where are you from?" Ben's mother asked. "The campsite right around the bend over there." "Okay, but where is your home?" Ben's mother asked. "Oh, my family lives in Alaska."

"Wow," Ben said, "Alaska, that's a million miles away. You must have used an awfully big sled to bring all that stuff with you!"

"No silly! We have a truck and trailer."

"Oh," Ben said with a frown on his face, "I was hoping to see your sled."

"We only have a toboggan for the winter, and that's just for fun." Shawn said.

"Okay, kids," Ben's mother laughed, "you guys can go play, but if you plan on leaving the area, you come tell me or your father, okay, Ben?"

"Okay, Mom, thanks."

The kids ran off to the water and tossed rocks into the lake. "Hey, Shawn, let's see who can skid the rocks the farthest."

"Sure, Ben. Hey, Ben, did you hear the story about the beast that lives in the forest?"

"No. What beast?" Ben asked with a fearsome expression.

"Well, supposedly there is a beast that lives in the forest, and he preys on humans. He is supposed to be really weird looking but almost looks like a dog. Some say like a large rat. They say he has a long nose and long tail and huge claws that can rip a human body to shreds! Some people have come out of the forest with horrific scratches and flesh hanging from their backs and arms and faces, and some people have never come out! No one has come close enough to see what it really looks like. The ones that have say that when it attacked them, it happened so fast that they never got to see it."

"OMG! Is this true, Shawn, or is this just a story to scare me?"

"No, really! It's true. Just last year, a little girl and her mother were exploring the forest and were seen running out of the woods screaming. The mother had scratches on her legs, and they swear it was a little beast."

"Has anyone ever gotten pictures of it?"

"No, it's kind of like the Loch Ness monster, Ogopogo, Sasquatch—no one really gets a good enough look or a picture, but they say this beast has been here for several hundred years. This campground has been here for twenty-five years, and the stories have been going around since they opened up here. The owners say its hearsay and that there is no proof of any kind. That the people that have come out of the woods have probably been attacked by a wolf or bear. I really think that they know more than they are telling us, but you can't blame them. This is their livelihood."

"OMG, my brother went in the woods this morning to explore! Should I tell my parents?"

"No, I wouldn't. You'll just worry them. No one has ever been killed by it—at least, there's no history of it. I would wait a while longer, and if he doesn't show up, then you should tell your parents. In the meantime, let's go for a swim, okay?"

"Sure, I'll race you to that buoy out there. Oh, wait a minute, Shawn. You're taller and older than me, so I should get a good head start before you, okay?"

"Sure, Ben, I'll give you a ten-foot start."

They swam around and played in the water for a while and when they pulled themselves out of the water, a friend of Shawn's showed up.

"Hey, Shawn, I wondered if your family would show up this year. We just got here twenty minutes ago. I told Mom and Dad that I was going to look for you."

"Hey, Lars, I can't believe you guys made it! We are going to have some fun this summer! Oh, by the way, this is my new friend, Ben. This is his first time here at the Hidden Woods."

"Hey, Ben, how's it going?"

"I was fine until Shawn told me about the killer animal in the forest. My brother is in there!"

"Oh, I wouldn't worry. Some people say it's just a story to keep guests coming to the campground, and others say that it is true. Myself, I have never met anyone that has come out injured, and my family has been coming here for ten years. So, Ben, I wouldn't worry."

Lars went over to Shawn. "I can't believe you told him that story, he's just a kid, and he'll probably have nightmares about it!"

"Well, I thought that I should warn him since his brother went exploring over an hour ago. I mean, if anything happens to his brother, I don't want to be the one that gets crap because I didn't mention the story."

Shawn looked over at Ben. "Hey, Ben, do you want to play soccer with Lars and me?"

"No, I think I'll go back to my campsite and have something to eat."

"Okay, maybe later then. Come on, Lars, I'll race ya."

CHAPTER

4

Matt finally awakens, rubbing his eyes and then stretching his arms over his head. "I feel like I've been sleeping for hours Geez, what time is it," he said as he dug in his pocket to find his mother's watch. "Where is it?" He searched and pulled the whites of his pockets out. "Must be in the other pocket." But he still came up empty-handed. "OMG, don't tell me I lost it. Mom is going to kill me. When did I unpin it?

"This can't be happening! I haven't even taken it out of my pocket. There is no way that it could come unpinned and fall out. I don't believe this!"

He started searching around the area where he had fallen asleep, his hands sifting through the ground's debris. Then he looked up and noticed that he was slowly losing daylight. "Boy, looking at the sun it must be heading for late afternoon, yet I haven't even had a chance to adventure or discover anything yet!"

Just then, he spotted a light flickering beyond in the woods.

"What is that?" he said as he moved his head from side to side to view between the trees.

Mysteriously, a yellow laser-like light is shining vibrantly through the shade of the pine trees, luring him to come check it out. Mystified, Matt got his belongings together and started to head in that direction. Dusk was only a few hours away, so he knew that he didn't have much time to check it out. He walked forward a ways and then looked back, a little nervous and unsure of what he was seeing or about to see. He questioned himself if he was smart to go off like this by himself, off the beaten trail. As he got a little closer to the brilliant laser light, he saw that it was the strange animal that he sat with earlier, and he had Matt's red watch dangling from his claws.

He followed it as far as it took him. "Hey, how did you get my watch? You give that back right now, or I'll kick your wiry little butt."

It just stared at him. It dropped his mother's watch, and it spoke again in a loud whisper, "***Over the bridge.***" His bulging eyes twinkled, his ears flapped, and he was gone. Just like that.

This is impossible. Animals can't speak. Unless . . . that was an alien. "I'm not afraid of you, whatever you are!" Matt yelled out to the sky with a slight squeal to his voice. "I'm not afraid of anything. Come on, show your face again!"

Matt was a little spooked, but the last thing he was going to do was show his fear to this . . . thing, whatever it was.

So he picked up his mother's watch and looked around as to where he was. He had no idea.

"I better get a move on it if I want to get back to the camp in time for dinner. I must have at least a one-and-a-half-hour walk if not more back to the camp."

Matt stopped and thought for a second. *What did he mean "over the bridge"? What is that supposed to mean. I have never heard a dog talk before, but is it a dog or an alien?*

The trail in front of him was distinct, very markable. There were rocks formed like small retaining walls. As he turned to look back, they were no longer there. It was just a regular pathway with ground debris.

As he looked forward, the path continued again, with the small rock walls on both sides of the path.

"Wow, this is really creepy! But I'm going to go see what's at the other end. Then tomorrow, I'm going to bring everyone back here to see this, because no one will believe me if they don't see it for themselves."

The flowers got larger and the smells stronger as he walked farther through the path. The pine and evergreen trees with their swooping large branches crossed over the pathway as the path swerved several times along the way from left to right and then back again. He looked up and saw this massive structure through a fog, a fog that was not there seconds ago. He could see several roof peaks pointing through the fog, and they looked gold or bronze.

"What is this?"

He looked back one more time to see if he could shake himself out of what he saw. When he turned forward again, it was still there, but now the fog was lifting—or in this case, the fog was falling. The fog was falling down toward the ground instead of lifting up. It all came toward the earth until it disappeared.

I have never seen fog do this before. This is starting to freak me out.

Matt was starting to get a little edgy and not really sure if he should continue going forward. But by the time the fog had completely dropped, he was in awe.

"**No way!** That's a **castle!**" Matt yelled out with excitement. "I am actually standing in front of a **castle! No freaking way!** Oh my god, it's so old and beautiful! I wonder how long it's been here. It must be hundreds of years old."

Matt was overjoyed. He never thought that in his **wildest dreams** he would ever see anything like this. This was over the top, and he was thrilled.

"I wonder if anyone owns it, or is it a haunted house? Maybe I'll just casually wander over the bridge, and if someone sees me, they will either tell me to get lost or ask me in. It would be so cool to see the inside of this place."

Matt walked closer to the bridge that hung over the moat and looked around in amazement.

"Wow, look at the moat around this place! It's so neat. I could stand on this bridge and fish here for hours. This must be what that scraggly little beast meant when he said *'Over the bridge.'* So then maybe there will be someone on the other side waiting for me."

Matt was hesitant for a few minutes but taking in the view at the same time. He had never seen a moat before, other than in pictures or storybooks. Never mind that he had never seen a castle before either—at least, not for real. The drawbridge was up, so he assumed that it meant that no one was home or it was empty. The breeze started to pick up again, this time a little stronger, and then a little stronger again. The breeze was strong enough to give him a mild push toward the drawbridge on the other side of the moat.

"Oh boy, I really want to go, but I don't know if I should."

And then a strong gust of wind blows by his ears and said *"Over the bridge! "*

Well, that scared Matt enough to start running over the bridge. He got to the end of the bridge over the moat and saw the drawbridge. It slowly started to lower with an awful, rusty creaking sound that was almost deafening to human ears. He put his hands over his ears and scrunched up his face. He had never heard anything so loud and painful before. The drawbridge made a loud thump when it rested on the ground.

Matt looked up with curiosity. "Now what? Someone must know that I'm here. Otherwise, how would the bridge know to come down?"

The castle stood out, so **gallant and soaring** like a giant, with its towers reaching the clouds. He counted at least five towers that he could see. It hurt his neck to look up so high. The towers had metal tops that looked like witches' hats. Yet there was also a lookout walkway around each tower. He thought that was probably where the guards used to hang out and watch for intruders coming, because from up there, you must have been able to see miles away.

"This place looks like it belonged in the medieval times."

Just then, he heard a soft and pleasant sound coming from the front door, but he was standing too far away to hear what it said. He went closer to the door to hear more clearly.

"Hello, are you talking to me?" Matt asked as he looked at the door, feeling a little foolish.

He grabbed the door knocker and hit it against the door three times, hoping someone would answer. Nothing, no one came. He was just about to pick up the door knocker again when he heard the voice.

"Make a wish as you enter," the voice whispered again. "What! This is a joke isn't it?"

He decided to say something to the door. Maybe someone would open it and allow him to enter.

"My name is Matt Franklin, and I just stumbled upon your castle. I was wondering if you would allow me to see your castle. It is so beautiful, like nothing I have ever seen before."

Nothing. The door did not open, and no one spoke. Matt didn't know if someone was playing a trick on him or not. He took a few steps backward and looked up as high as he could again, but there was no one there. He looked toward the bridge over the moat. No one there.

He looked at his watch and saw that it was 4:30 p.m.

"Oh crap, I had better start heading back to the campsite. I don't want to get in trouble for not being back on time. I can always come back tomorrow with friends. Ya, maybe it's a better idea to try and get inside this castle with someone else. At least then I can have a look out while I go in."

As he took a few steps away from the castle, the voice spoke yet again, **"Make a wish as you enter."**

"Seriously? Okay, I'll play the game, but I only have a half hour, then I have to go."

So Matt put his hands on the elegant yet rugged Gothic cast-iron door handle in the shape of a rose, which had an extremely warm feel to it.

He thought, *What am I supposed to wish for?*

Again he heard the voice. **"Make a wish as you enter."**

"Okay, okay! I'm thinking. You're not giving me much time to think." *I'm at the front door of an old castle probably of medieval times. Hmm. Okay. I think I know.* "I wish I could spend my holiday in a medieval life. Oh, and I also would like to try out a jet plane." *Hehe, now let's see them pull that one off. Hehehe.*

He slowly opened the old-world doors made of solid wood, and it took almost all of his strength just to get them opened. He found himself inside the castle and was almost overcome by what happened next.

CHAPTER

5

"Good den, my lord," a female flight attendant addressed Matt. "What?" Matt whispered.

"Sir Matthew, thou art now entering a different dimension, one that time hath not forgotten, only misplaced."

"I don't understand."

"In good time, Sir Matthew, in good time."

"I'm really thirsty, miss. Could you bring me something to drink?" "Indeed, Sir Matthew, what would thou like?"

"How do you know my name? And its Matt, no one calls me Matthew ever!" he says with anxiety in his voice while he pinches the skin on his arm to try to wake up from this dream.

"Art thou feeling all right, Sir Matthew? Perhaps thou had an odd dream, which is not unusual. Dost thou need to use the privy?"

"What is a privy?" Matt asked.

"A privy is a place where thou canst wash up. Anyways, I shall get thy orange juice with a little spirits for thee, and stop pinching thine arm, thee shalt have red marks all over thee, and if this happens, how shall I explain it to the king and queen?"

How does she know I wanted orange juice, and how does she know my name?

King and queen! *What the heck is going on here?*

Matt was starting to get really nervous. He didn't know where he was or how he got on the plane. A woman he had never seen before called him by his name and told him not to pinch his skin or she'd have to explain it to the king and queen. "*What king and queen?* Miss, miss!" He waved his hand, trying to get her attention.

"Hither, Sir Matthew, thy orange juice with a little spirits. Is thither something thou want to bid me?"

"No, but I want to ask you something."

The flight attendant laughed and then said, "Certainly, go ahead."

"Um, ya, first of all, what language are you talking? It sounds like broken English. And what the heck are you talking about? King and queen, what king and queen? You're talking like I'm royalty or something! And you're freaking me out big time! And how did I get on this plane? I'm starting to get really spooked here! And if you know what's going on, then you have an obligation to tell me, and stop calling me Sir Matthew!"

"A lot of questions for such a young lad. All in good time, all in good time, Sir Matthew, and it shall all make sense to thee once thou hath departed from the airplane. In the meantime, sit back and take pleasure in the sights outside the window. It may be a long time before thou art able to see such magnificence again, and remember, Sir Matthew, 'tis was thy wish that brought thee to us." The airplane attendant said with such a tranquil, gentle tone as she walked away.

Am I going crazy? The way she speaks is so bizarre, and I still don't know what's going on here! Matt looked around the plane to see if he recognized anyone. The plane was a large one, but there were no more than ten people on it. He wondered if he should go talk to someone to find out where the plane was going and if they also noticed weirdness about this voyage. He was sitting beside the window and stretched over the extra two seats to look down the aisle. Then he decided no, he would stay where he was and let things unfold as they would.

The female attendant came back to reassure Matt that there was nothing to be troubled about, that he was in superior hands, that he would have the time of his life for the next few days, and that before departing the aircraft, she would give him a few lessons on *the old English language*. It would aid him in preparation for his journey.

"Miss," Matt said quietly, "these other people on the plane, are we all going to the same place?"

"Oh no, Sir Matthew, certainly not. Each of you hath thine own wishes and dreams."

She also told him that this was all that she was authorized to discuss. She tenderly caressed his cheek with her soft, lavender-scented hand and smiled as she walked away.

Matt blushed as she walked away, and he was beginning to really like her. She certainly made him feel calmer.

Gosh, the last thing I remember is saying a wish at the castle door. Could this, in fact, be real and not a dream or hallucination? This is magical and thrilling all at the same time! OMG! My wish really came true! No one is going to believe me when I tell them. I just know it!

Matt decided to take the airplane attendant's suggestion by sitting back and taking in the magnificence in the sights below. He just stared out the window and was mesmerized by what he saw. They were flying at only five hundred feet above ground, so he was able to see everything below.

He got glimpses of flourishing meadows in radiant colors of greens and browns, with gentle rolling hills and farm lands and forests. He saw peaks of rooftops and crowns of castles beyond the meadows. There were folks on horses, folks just doing nothing, kids playing with their families and their pets, and livestock roaming around. He spotted white and yellow daisies as well as lavender-tinted flowers just scattered far and wide. They looked like clusters of dots in all places. They were magnificent.

As the plane got closer to the ground, he became thrilled and anxious at the same time. He wanted off the plane now! He started jumping in his seat like a little boy seeing a Christmas tree jam-packed with presents.

"Hold on to thine britches, Sir Matthew. The plane must land before thou canst depart!" the attendant shouted.

"Boy, there is a lot going on down there and so much to see! Where are we?" he asked the attendant.

"Thou shalt be given all the knowledge that thee seeks before thou departs the plane," the attendant said in a gracious manner.

"Huh!"

"It is time thou knowest ye Olde English," the attendant said as she sat down beside Matt.

Matt was all ears for her and eager to be taught.

"Do as thou wilts, but in order for good gentles and ladies not to laugh at thou, I shall teach thee some words and phrases." She sat next to Matt.

"First and foremost, addressing the king and queen, Your Majesty or Your Highness. I ask you, I bid you. What's your name, what be your name? Good-bye, my friend; fare thee well, my goodman. Good-bye, ladies; adieu, my good ladies. *You* is either *thou* or *thee. Your, thine* or *thy. There, thither. Can, canst.* Where is the restroom, whither is the privy? Come here, come hither. What did you say, what say you?

"Now, Sir Matthew, the language hath not changed considerably. Thee shant have much trouble."

"Wow, I hope I don't mess up!" Matt said.

"Methinks not," the attendant said as she got up from the seat and walked away.

The plane started to gradually descend. Matt was captivated as he watched out the miniature porthole, seeing the earth getting nearer and nearer to him. Then he felt a firm bump beneath him. It was the plane, and the wheels hit ground. The sound of the engine flaps breaking the speed frightened him, and he cringed as he hung on to his seat. The plane felt like it was going too fast to stop.

The attendant looked over at Matt and gave him a big smile. Matt was somewhat reassured by her gesture. Her smile reminded him of his own mother and how she always gave him a big smile when he was afraid.

The plane came to a screeching halt.

"We're here!" Matt yelled out and let out a huge sigh of relief.

The attendant came over to Matt, took his hand and walked him to the exit door.

"Am I going out alone?"

"Yea, Sir Matthew, this is thine wish and thine alone. Dost not be afraid. Be strong and manly, and methinks thee shalt have a splendid time."

"Can you at least tell me where I am?"

"Yea, Sir Matthew. Thou art in Britain. Fare thee well, my goodman,"

And with that, the exit door swung open, and the attendant put her hand on Matt's shoulder and gave him a gentle shove forward.

Matt walked down the stairs from the plane. The sun was shining fiercely, and it was so bright that he could not see anything in front of him. When he got to the bottom of the step, he looked back to wave at the attendant. He was horror-struck when he saw that the airplane was already gone.

CHAPTER

"It's gone, it's all gone!" Matt shrieked. Then he realized this was a fantasy or a wish, because this just couldn't happen in real life.

He started to calm down a little bit. He looked all around, looked at the luscious green grass that surrounded him. He looked at the giant green trees that hovered above him. He looked at the meadows beyond with the stunning flowers that showed splendor in their colors, the way the hills rolled and the tall grasses swayed through the meadow. He noticed the creek beyond with the water thrusting through it like torrents. There were some chickens running around and some trying to take flight. Then he looked up at the superb turquoise painted sky with not a cloud in sight. The warm sun on his face completed the amazing sensation he was receiving. He had a triumphant smile on his face, kind of like a smile of achievement. He felt great. He sat down in the field against a large rock. He leaned his head back next to the rock and just closed his eyes and breathed in that sweet air, feeling the warmth of the sun on his face caressing him back into a sleep again, that feel of the pleasant breeze like fingers going through his hair.

He had fallen asleep for a good hour and was just starting to come around when he heard some movement behind him, some feet crunching through the large grasses. He wondered who he would encounter next.

"Man, no one is going to believe me when I get back home. I have to find something I can take with me from here to prove to my friends and family that this isn't bogus. This is real!" He looked around, talking to himself.

The sounds were getting closer. He heard several pairs of feet, and then he heard a voice—a male voice, most likely in his teens. And he could hear a few more voices behind him, also coming his way.

"Matthew? Matthew? Is that thee, sitting against the rock over yonder?" the strange voice asks.

How the heck does he know my name? OMG, could this be a former life that I lived and am revisiting? This is so confusing, but I am having a great time with it. I can do whatever I want, go to bed when I want, eat when I want. Whatever I want, I hope."

Little did Matt know that this was not quite the fantasy that he had envisioned.

The voices that he was hearing were getting closer upon him. Matt started to look around both sides of the rock he was leaning against to see who it was.

"Matthew? Matthew! It is thee, and what in damnation art thou wearing? Thou art almost naked!"

Matt looked down at himself, afraid of what he would see, but he still had his jean shorts on and blue socks and white runners with red laces and his T-shirt with the Spiderman insignia on it.

"No, I'm not almost naked. I'm wearing my summer clothes."

"Summer clothes?" the other boy questioned. "What are summer clothes?" "You're joking, aren't you?" Matt asked.

"Joke? Goodman, how fare thee?" he asked.

"Oh, I remember what that means. The flight attendant taught me some of your language. I'm doing fine. By the way, what's your name?"

"Oh, Matthew, I bid you, hast thee fallen and hit thine noggin? Methinks ye art not well. I am thy best friend, Jacob. Come, we must take thee to the town leech!"

"Leech? What the heck is a leech?" Matt yelled, and he was a little nervous with that word, because he knew what a leech was, but did it have the same meaning for Jacob?

"The town healer," Jacob had a troubled look on his face. He was concerned about his friend Matthew.

"I'm not sick! I'm perfectly fine," Matt said with a pitchy tone of voice.

"Splendid! Then we must leave now! And find you another attire," Jacob said with a frantic tone.

Both Jacob and the other boys, Fredrick and Lester, grabbed Matt by the arms and pulled him off the ground. As they pulled him up, Jacob said to Matt with an anxious manner. "Matthew, we must first bring thee to safety and then change thou attire."

"What do you mean bring me to safety? Am I in some sort of trouble?" Matt was confused.

Frederick and Lester both jumped in at about the same time, yelling, "Dost thou not remember? Thy brother is out to kill thee!"

"Why? Did I steal his Wii game?" Matt asked with a giggle and a smirk on his face.

"Wii? What is this Wii game?" a baffled Lester asked.

"Oh ya, I forgot. You haven't seen the future, have you?" Matt quietly said to himself. "Forget it, Lester. I don't think I have time to explain the Wii system to you. Maybe later."

"Come we have no more time to waste!" Jacob yelled.

They all ran through the meadows, down the hill, and through the wooded lands until they found a safe area to stop and catch their breaths.

Matt, panting, said, "Tell me again, who wants to kill me?" "Thy brother," said Jacob, panting as well.

"Ben? Ben is here too?" Matt was stunned.

"Nay," Jacob said. "Thy brother, Isaiah. Have thee gone completely mad, Matthew?"

"Okay, I'm new to this. Remind me why my brother Isaiah wants to kill me? And when you say kill me, you mean beat the crap out of me, right?" Matt said with a teasing form.

Jacob looked over at Frederick and Lester with a dismal look on his face. "Men, methinks Sir Matthew needest our help more than methinks. Methinks something hast fallen on his noggin and perhaps done some damage."

They all agreed with Jacob and shook their heads with sadness.

"Sir Matthew, thou art next in line for the throne! Isaiah, thy brother, is out to behead thee so that he will be next in line for the throne. Dost thee understand me?" Jacob said with a worried tone to his voice.

"Verily, it is so," Lester said.

"Ye must listen to us, Sir Matthew! We must get thee to the sanctuary where thou can claim the right of the sanctuary for forty days," Fredrick stated.

"Fredrick!" Lester yelled. "By my troth, thou art a boil! Sir Matthew is not a fugitive! We cannot seek the help of the sanctuary!"

"Yea, if we let it be known that we have a fugitive in custody, then he will be safe for forty days until we find somewhere else for him to hide." Frederick said with excitement.

"My goodmen," Jacob said, "dost thee remember that someone must stand guard outside the church to ensure Sir Matthew's safety?"

"We shalt take turns until we find elsewhere for him to hide," Frederick stated.

"'Tis most splendid. If all are in agreement, then say thee yea," Jacob said to the other boys.

All three of them said yea together and then patted Matt on the back and shoulder.

"We shall make sure nothing happens to thee, Sir Matthew, by my troth!" Jacob said with trust in his tone.

"So when you say I am next in line for the throne, does that mean that my parents are king and queen?" Matt questioned with excitement in his voice.

"Yea, Matthew. Ye is the eldest and His Majesty is dying. He has polio. The medicines art not working anymore. His Majesty may have only days to live." Jacob said with sadness in his voice.

"If thy brother Isaiah kills thee before His Majesty dies then he is next in line to be king, and that, my goodman, wilt destroy us all, and war would be eminent," Frederick said with grief.

"Why does no one like Isaiah? Is he mean? What is it? Help me to understand," Matt said.

"We shalt explain everything to thee when we get thee to the sanctuary!" Jacob said with urgency in his voice.

"Let us go thither *now*!" Jacob yelled.

The sanctuary was a good twenty-five-minute sprint for the boys. They were outside the town, which meant they had to cross the moat to get into the village to avoid being seen with Matt. His brother, Isaiah, had been on the lookout for him, and Isaiah had numerous spies working for him, so they had to be extra vigilant.

With Matthew dressed in jean shorts, a Spiderman T-shirt, green socks and white runners with red laces, he was totally out of place. The boys had to enclose Matthew when they were exposed to other villagers who were out on their daily stroll or working the fields.

The boys noticed a grouping of maidens sitting under an oak tree. One of the maidens was reading from a parchment to the others as one of them noticed the boys and started to giggle. She bashfully looked at the boys and pointed in their direction, and the other maidens turned to look at them. The boys realized they had been spotted, so they threw themselves on top of Matthew to hide him from view.

"Hey!" Matthew yelled. "Damn you, guys. What the heck are you doing? You can't just throw me down like that and dog pile me. At least give me notice, you bunch of jackasses!"

"Shush!" whispered Jacob, "Alack! Over yonder art some wenches, and methinks they have spotted us. Stay."

The maiden who was reading to the other girls casually started to walk over to the boys.

"Good den," the maiden said to the boys with a smile. "How fare thee?"

She was a little concerned because they were all lying on the ground, sprawled out on top of each other, with Matthew lying on the bottom in such a way that he could not be spotted except for the red laces on his running shoes.

Jacob smiled back at her, a little embarrassed, not just because of their situation but also because he had seen her numerous times in town and he had eyes for her.

"Ahhh," he said, stumbling for words to say, "excellent well. Grammercy."

"I have been admiring thee. Ye art quite handsome," she said with friskiness in her voice. She was upfront with Jacob with no apprehension at all.

Jacob's face went several shades of red, and the other boys laughed and poked him in the side, which prompted him to speak without thinking.

"I like thine face, and I applaud thine effort," Jacob rambled out. He couldn't believe what he had just said and hoped that the maiden would not fault him for his tongue.

The boys and maidens all laughed hysterically. Poor Jacob was outright embarrassed and, at that moment, wished he was dead.

"Do not fret," the maiden said. "I do not judge on our first meet."

"What be your name, sweet mistress?" Jacob once again could not believe he said that to her. He was smitten by her, and no matter what he wanted to say, it just did not come out right.

Frederick, Lester, and Matt were now laughing so hard they had tears in their eyes, and they were stirring around way too much for Jacob's liking. Matthew's shoes were showing from underneath the bodies. Jacob noticed this and positioned his back over Matt's feet when he heard a yell.

"*Ouch*, you jerk!"

"Tiffany is my name, and what be your name?" "Jacob," he said with a crackle in his voice.

"Pray tell, art those not another set of feet under thine back?" She was pointing to Matt's feet. "And this extra set of feet, to whom do they belong to?" Tiffany asked with a smile on her face and a chuckle in her voice.

Now, Jacob did not know what to say. He looked over at Frederick and Lester. They looked the other way, and Lester put his hand over Matt's mouth so that he could not speak any more.

"Well, my lady," Jacob started to stutter. "Ye must be mistaken. Thither art no extra set of feet. Thine beautiful emerald eyes must be playing tricks. 'Tis only Frederick and Lester, my goodmen, and I. Perchance thine eyes hath seen a ghost of sorts."

Tiffany rolled her eyes at Jacob. She knew he was hiding something but decided to let them play their little game and pretend that she believed him. It is always best to permit the male to believe that he had won the battle in order to keep him flustering when in his presence she felt. She decided that she would keep her eye on him and his company.

CHAPTER

7

The boys made it to the entrance to the village without being spotted a second time. The landscaping around the village was surrounded by a moat, which was very deep, with walls made of stone. The walls had battlements at the tops with eighteen towers built into these walls, and there were archers at the tops of these walls, between the battlements, who would keep watch for trespassers. The access gate was opened so the boys wouldn't have any difficulty entering. The guards closed the gate at night, so it was almost impossible to enter at night unless you had permission. The drawbridge was made of wood and hinged in a way so that it could be moved parallel to the ground. They walked as calmly as they could across the bridge in a laid-back manner so they would not be suspected of any wrong.

The town followed the contour of a riverbank, and as a result of this they had steep and meandering streets with irregular widths. The land was limited within the walls of the town, and the only access in and out of town was the main street that ran through the village and to the village gate.

The streets were crowded and full of obstacles such as street vendors, horsemen, and iron workers. Pigs were running wildly through the streets. Most people kept a pig because they were a cheap and good source of food; however, houses were small, so pigs were let out into the streets to scavenge. There was a village stage, taverns, blacksmiths, and barbers. Some had storefronts, and some were working in the streets. There was an area sectioned off for fights between animals, which were part of the medieval entertainment—wild animals against each other or trained dogs fighting lions, tigers, bears, and bulls. Matt's head was spinning as he was taking this all in. Everything was going past his eyes too quickly as the boys dragged him inconspicuously to the sanctuary.

The town was very picturesque, and Matt wanted to slow down. He wanted to enjoy the sights, but the boys wouldn't agree to it. They had to get Matt to safety.

"Sir Matthew," Jacob said, "we must get thee to the sanctuary immediately. Then we will grace thee with some attire and a feast."

"Well, how much farther do we have to go? I'm getting awfully tired," Matt said exhaustedly.

"It is over yonder, my goodman," spoke Jacob. "Sir Matthew, I bid you, wherefore dost thee speak in this manner? Thee must keep quiet and not speak to strangers, or they shalt think thee is an airling."

"What's an airling?" Matt asked.

"An airling." Lester pointed to Matt's head and said "Empty."

The boys all chuckled as they continued down the cobble road to the sanctuary. Frederick had picked up a cloak that he found hanging on the saddle of a horse and had put it around Matt's shoulders to cover his twenty-first-century clothing.

They walked through some extremely narrow streets. Matt was amazed. He could almost touch buildings on both sides of the street at the same time if he stretched his arms out as far as they could go and added another two to three feet to either side.

"Come, my goodmen, we must move apace," said Jacob as they huddled closer to Matt and pushed the back of his head to keep it in the downward position.

They finally reached the church. It had a name inscribed above the doorway, Saint Mary's 1469. It had an ironbound door standing fourteen feet tall. Entering the cathedral, Matt saw a grotesque brass door knocker. It was the hideous mask of a beast. It was a reminder to the fugitive of the awful fate that was in store for him if he entered this sanctuary.

"Hey, guys, what's with the ugly door knocker? What does it mean?" Matt questioned.

"Anon, we enter first, and then we shalt explain all thither is to know about this sanctuary to thee, Sir Matthew," Fredrick said.

They knocked on the door several times until a man of the cloth answered the door. He looked at them in surprise. "What needest thou, my lads?" he asked.

Jacob spoke first. "Good den, Your Worship. We have a most unusual beseech."

"Well, on with it, my lad," the man of the cloth said with haste in his voice.

At this point Jacob decided to tell the minister the truth about Matt being stalked by his brother, instead of pretending that Matt was a criminal, as that could cause more hardship, and he hoped that they would be obliged.

"This young lad hither is Sir Matthew, son of His Majesty Vincent and Her Highness Julianne. We must keep him hidden, as his brother, Sir Isaiah, is out to behead Sir Matthew, as he is next in line for the throne."

Joshua, who was minister of the church, was shocked when they introduced Matt to him. He quickly opened the doors wide and escorted them in. "Come quickly," Joshua said. "Have thee spotted Sir Isaiah yet?"

"Nay," said the boys.

"Methinks thou shalt find Sir Matthew another place to hide soon. This is not a place for him. I shalt help thee, Sir Matthew. It would be my honour," Joshua said with pride.

"A fie this is!" Joshua spoke and looked directly at Matt. "Thou art the son and heir of a mongrel bitch! Thy mother, Her Highness Julianne, hath put Isaiah first and above thee since he was born. Methinks she hath put Isaiah up to this. Worry not Sir Matthew, we shall protect thee!"

"Yea!" the three boys and the minster yelled out at once. "First we must collect some trousers and a tunic," Jacob said.

The boys and the minister dug around and came up with a dark yellow tunic (which was like wearing a mini dress) with a white belt and a pair of flaxen Norman trousers in red with leather lacing that wrapped around his ankle upward to just under his knees. Then they gave him a pair of short leather Celtic ankle boots with leather laces.

"You're kidding right?" Matt said with an uncertain tone to his voice. "I will look gay!"

"Then gay ye shall be," said Joshua.

"Oh crap," Matt mumbled under his breath.

"Sir Matthew, enow prating and dress up. Once thou is done, I shalt show thee this sanctuary, and we shalt have a feast, for we art famished," Jacob said.

Matt grabbed the clothes, went behind a drape, and got changed. Everything seemed to fit appealingly well. He looked in a mirror and liked what he saw.

"Boy, I kind of like the clothes these people wear. I know if I wore something like this at home, I'd get razzed and probably beat up. I wish I had a camera with me. I'll ask them to hide my clothes so no one throws them out or steals them so when I go back home I can put them back on."

Matt walked out past the drape and asked the minister if he could store his clothes for him. Then he walked up to Jacob and asked him, "What say you we eat now?" (He was trying out his new English.)

"Ah, Sir Matthew, ye English is coming back, goodman. Joshua is fetching us some grub, cometh with me, and I shall show ye this sanctuary."

All three boys walked together with Matt and showed him around the church. As they walked around, Matt had several questions, and Jacob gave him all the insight that he needed.

"Hey, Jacob, what's with those men over there with the black robes on?" "I shall start at the beginning, Sir Matthew."

Jacob began to tell Matt that the people held up in the sanctuary were adulterers, horse stealers, forgers of the kings' coinage, and most of all, murderers. A criminal had a short period of time to decide whether to give himself up to local authorities and face trial and punishment or confess his crimes and beg for forgiveness. A fugitive would be stripped and made to wear a plain black garment that bore the symbol of a yellow cross on his left breast. Charity in the form of simple food and drink was provided, but not until after his confession countdown began. The fugitive admitting his guilt to God and the authorities had thirty-seven days to leave England forever by sea. If he ever tried to return, he would be put to death.

Jacob and the boys brought him to the altar, which was the holiest of places. The altar had three gothic arches with stained glass in each in the form of a five-petal rose. Matt was astounded by the workmanship, for they didn't have the tools that we had in the twenty-first century.

"I thought it was safe here for anyone up to forty days? And should I really be here? I mean, it sounds like it's a jail for criminals. Do these people know who I am? And am I safe here from these people?" Matt asked.

"Not to worry, Sir Matthew. All who enter this sanctuary are safe, even from each other. Some have been hither for forty days and others for thirty-seven. No one knows thee, Sir Matthew, and we shalt keep it that way. From hither forward ye art Jacob's brother. We shall no longer call you *sir*," said Frederick.

"That's fine by me. I can't get used to people calling me *sir*," Matt said.

Joshua had a large feast set up for the boys and called them over to come eat. The table was covered with a white silk cloth. At home, Matt's mom covered the table with placemats. She would never use silk—they couldn't afford it, and even if they could, she would save it for company. There were silver candlesticks on the table, and they illuminated the spacious hall where the table was set up. The platters were made of pewter. There were silver dishes, cups, and saltshakers that were in the shapes of dogs. The drinking cups were made of wood, which was very unusual to Matt. He never drank from wood before, but he felt like a king just sitting at this table.

A servant came around the table with a basin full of water for each to wash their hands in before dinner. The water even had a perfume smell to it. After he washed his hands, he was given a napkin to dry his hands with. They were served broths, soups that were highly seasoned with spice, potages, ragouts, hashes, and roasted meat, and the fish consisted of red herring, white herring, sturgeon, and stockfish.

Matt was getting dizzy watching all the food being dropped onto the table. It kept going on and on. There were herring pies, morsels of whale, beef, pork, and duck and fowl, and last but not least, bread. Then they brought the red wine. He wasn't sure if he should drink it because he had tried it a couple of times and it made him lightheaded, or as his new friends said, airling. Most of the food that was served made him cringe at the sight of them, so he ate what was recognizable to him.

They sat at the table for over an hour, eating, drinking, laughing, and storytelling, and then Jacob stood up and said, "I shall see you anon. I must go search for a certain maiden. Frederick and Lester, thou shall stay with Matthew until I return."

CHAPTER

8

"So, guys, now tell me why my brother Isaiah is out to kill me, other than he wants to be next in line for the throne. I sure as hell don't want to die, but what's up with him, what's his problem, why can't he accept that I am the rightful heir to the throne and wait until I don't want it anymore?"

Joshua answered Matt with seriousness in his tone. "Sir Matthew, ye dost not understand. Thine brother Isaiah is evil. We cannot allow him to take over the throne or the government of this village. He hath killed scores of village people merely because they wouldst not give him a good price on silks and other riches. Isaiah lives to kill and needs the throne to have all worship him."

"Joshua!" Fredrick addressed him with haste. "Hast thee forgotten Sir Matthew hast fallen and hit his head? He cannot remember."

"Ah aye," Joshua remembered. "Okay, I shall fill ye in on the history and mayhap shall bring back some memory."

Matt got himself comfortable at the table and grabbed another goblet of wine as they all sat and listened to Joshua explain to Matt of the problems they faced.

Joshua began with the story. "A sequence of bloody wars termed the **Wars of the Roses** hath broke out in 1455. It hath been pushed by an economic crisis and a common awareness of poor government. The Yorkists removed Henry from power in 1461, but by 1469, fighting recommenced as Edward, Henry, and Edward's brother George, backed by leading nobles and powerful French followers, vied for power.

"By 1471, Edward wert victorious and most of his rivals were dead. On his death, power passed to his brother Richard of Gloucester, who at first ruled on behalf of the young Edward V before seizing the throne himself as Richard III. The future Henry VII, aided by French and Scottish troops, returned to England and defeated Richard at the Battle of Bosworth in 1485, bringing an end to the majority of the fighting.

"Thither hath not been a war since. We art afraid that this shall cometh to an end. You see, Matthew, thy father, His Majesty Vincent, married thy stepmother, her Lady Juliann, under protest. He wert still grief stricken with the death of thy true mother, Her Highness Patricia, when he hath met with thy stepmother, he was a tosspot, and well, one thing led to another, although many of the villagers believe she coerced him, maybe even drugged him. A few weeks later, she was with child, so His Majesty Vincent hath no option but to taketh her hand in marriage. Thus, she became royalty through marriage. It was a ploy so she could get what she wanted.

"Her family wert dirty scoundrels. They cheated and stole from the villagers. They hath money, but the one thing they hath not wert royal blood. The only way to get this was through marriage, which Juliann accomplished. Once she got her own son to the throne, her family was set to rule the village and take ownership of all the people that lived within the walls of the village. No one would ever own a home again or a business. They would be paid by the Royals a small peasant's salary and would make the Royals one of the richest in all of Britain.

"Nine months later, thy half brother was born, but thou wert thy father's son. Thy mother could not stand the looks of thee because thou was so close to thy father, and thy father hath no interest in a child that he hath not wanted. Thy brother Isaiah was coddled by thy stepmother. She hath known that thy father hath no interest in Isaiah and wert afraid that this couldst hurt her future. He wert going to be the child that Juliann would mold to fit her needs, her family's needs.

"Thee, Matthew, art like thy father: kind, understanding, giving. Thee hath a heart of gold. Thy father and thee hath always been so close, unlike Isaiah—he is thy stepmother's child. He doth all that she asks of him and never questions anything. Thy father and stepmother hath not slept together for many, many years. They dost not speaketh to each other unless they must."

"Wait a minute," Matt said. "How do you know all of this?"

"Thy father and I hath grown up together as lads. He hath always confided in me, and he tells me his sorrows and his confessions. Now this stays here between thou and I. No one is to know any of this! If any of this gets out of this sanctuary, there could be death among us!" Joshua said with uneasiness in his voice.

"Not to worry, Joshua, my lips are sealed," Matt said.

"So now, thy father is dying, and with thee next in line thou is a threat to thy stepmother and Isaiah. Their plan is to eliminate thee so that Isaiah can take the throne and do as his mother orders," Joshua said with deep sadness in his voice.

"So dost thee understand now, Sir Matthew, that if Isaiah has the throne, then there will be an imminent outbreak in war? There hath been no threat until Her Highness Juliann and Sir Isaiah," Joshua said with exhaustion in his voice.

"Wow" was all Matt could say.

Fredrick spoke up. "We must keep thee safe until thine father passes and even then we shalt have guards with thee at all times."

"But I can't live like I'm a prisoner, and I'll be going home soon, so what we have to do is find a way to strip my stepmother and stepbrother of their titles at the same time," Matt said with excitement.

"And how dost thee thinks we shall do this?" Jacob asks.

"Well, let me think a moment. If we can find a way for all of the villagers to hear the truth about my stepmother and brother, and if my father has to sign a document telling the villagers that if something were to happen to me, then the throne would not go to my brother or stepmother, but to have a vote amongst the villagers as to who they would believe to be most trustworthy to sit in power and then they can vote." Matt said with such anticipation in his voice. He felt like an adult.

"Sir Matthew, the villagers have not ever had a vote for anything. This is left up to the council, and only royal blood can inherit the throne," Joshua said.

"Well, then maybe it's time to change things," Matt strongly stated.

* * * *

"Lester, whither hath ye been?" Frederick asked with distress in his voice. "Joshua hath told Matthew the plight we art all in since two hours after midday."

"I went to fetch some water, and then I used the privy," Lester said as if he needed approval from Frederick. "I wert coming back this way. I heard a ruckus out back, so I opened the postern behind the eating quarters. I carefully opened it, and to my astonishment, thither he be, Sir Isaiah, with his goons."

"Did he spot you, Lester?" Frederick asked, horrified, as all eyes were staring at Lester.

"Nay he hath not, but for Sir Isaiah to be outside the sanctuary, he must hath some mistrust. It doth worrit me so," Lester said with anxiety.

"Okay, we must not become foolish at this time. No matter what, we must protect Sir Matthew or our lives will cometh to an end as we see it," spoke Joshua with apprehension.

There was a loud echoing thump at the sanctuary door. Lester, Frederick, Joshua, and Matt all froze and stared at each other. The expressions on their faces looked horrifying.

"Frederick and Lester, ye must taketh Matthew to the dungeon and hide him. Dost not leave the sanctuary grounds until I cometh to fetch ye," Joshua whispered with worry.

"Okay, Joshua, dost not give us away with the fright in your face," Frederick said.

There were four louder thumps at the sanctuary door. Joshua looked back to make sure the boys were out of sight before he opened the doors.

The three boys ran as hard as they could through the hall and down the three flights of stairs. They had to be as quiet as they possibly could because everything echoed within the sanctuary walls. They came to a crossroads—there were three hallways with a roundabout in the middle that Joshua had forgotten to tell them about. They gazed at one another for a second or two as to which one to take. Then Frederick took leadership and ran to the one to their left, and Lester and Matthew followed and ran, for their lives depended on it.

It felt like there was no end to this dungeon hall. It was smelly and wet, and there were rats running about. The boys got spooked many times but tried to ignore their fears. What was important was for Matt not to be spotted. He was the most important thing at that moment, and no one could harm him.

What the boys didn't realize was this dungeon hall was leading them through a secret underground tunnel that ran through the village. It was built over one hundred years ago by prisoners who had escaped their fate. Not many people knew about this, which was a good thing for the boys.

Matt stumbled and was holding his stomach. He started to retch.

"Sir Matthew, we cannot stay. The stench hither shall make thee retch more so. We must keep running," Lester yelled quietly.

But Matt couldn't. He keeled over and started to throw up. He wasn't used to the grotesque smell of decaying rats and the musty dungeon. He couldn't go on, and he couldn't stop throwing up. All that nasty food that he ate was spewing out of his throat.

Frederick and Lester grabbed Matt by the arms. They put him in the middle of them, and between them two, they carried him off as he was still retching his guts out. Matt noticed the rats coming out from under the cement walls and running toward what Matt had vomited on the ground. He was so disgusted that at that moment he just wanted to be at home in his clean, fresh-smelling bed. He knew that wasn't going to happen so he had to pull himself together and keep moving forward.

* * * *

Joshua waited until the boys had a five-minute start. In the meantime, Isaiah and his mob kept banging on the heavy doors until they were answered.

Joshua slowly opened the doors and saw Isaiah and five of his hooligans standing there.

"Sir Isaiah, it has been a goodly length in times past since I have laid mine eyes upon thee," Joshua said with tension in his voice.

"Aye. I am in search for my brother, Sir Matthew. Our father has beseeched for him to cometh to his deathbed," Isaiah said with command.

"But why art thee hither? Why would Sir Matthew needest to come hither?" Joshua asked. He was trying to stall them for as long as he possibly could. "His Majesty Vincent is a verily dear goodman of mine. Perchance I shall say my adieu to him," Joshua said with heavy heart.

"Do as thou wilts," Isaiah said with annoyance. "I am hither for Sir Matthew. Whither is he?"

"I have not seen Sir Matthew since he was a small lad." Joshua said hoping that Isaiah would not see through his lies.

Isaiah and his gang pushed their way through the door, pushing Joshua aside, almost knocking him to the ground.

"I bid you once more. Whither is Matthew? Ye durst not forswear to me! I have a spy that saith Sir Matthew wert brought into the sanctuary. By my troth, if ye forswear me, I wilts make ye one of the wooden gnomes of the woods!" Isaiah shouted in anger.

By now, Joshua was becoming extremely threatened. The Royal family was known for having supernatural powers, and he couldn't trust Isaiah to spare his life, even though he was a close friend of his father. Anyone who betrayed Isaiah became a wooden gnome figure in the forest. He had them scattered throughout the woods as reminders to the villagers not to cross him. He had even cursed his uncle with his mother's blessing.

"Prithee, Sir Isaiah, by my troth, I have not seen Sir Matthew, I have not been out of the cooks' cellar all day. I dost not see many in a day. Perchance they hath cometh through the doors by another. If thou wouldst care, thou canst walk through the sanctuary to see with thine own eyes," Joshua cowardly pleaded.

"Stay thy prating!" Isaiah yelled as he and his troops marched through the sanctuary, all spread out, each of the six of them all taking different routes. They were there to capture and kill. Joshua could see in their faces that the search had nothing to do with his father dying, because Isaiah could care less. They were there to capture his brother, Matthew, and put a dagger through his heart. There was never any brotherly love between the two. Matthew, being the older brother, was his father's favourite. Also Matthew was the king's true son with the woman he had always loved and will always love—Matthew's mother, Patricia. For the king to have two sons and one preferred over the other was not just demeaning to Isaiah but made him worthless as the king's son. His mother kept forcing this upon Isaiah and had him believe that his father hated him and that the only way that he could become king and her (Juliann) heir to the kingdom was to have the eldest son killed, so that when their father, His Majesty, died, Isaiah would become king by right. Then they would be the rulers of the village. Even Juliann thought it would be fitting to have the king and his firstborn son buried together.

Joshua stood there in shock, praying that the boys would find the secret corridor and get out of this mess, because if they were caught, it would be imminent death for Sir Matthew, and as for the other two well, they would be in the **ring of doom.**

Isaiah yelled to his gang, "**Spread out down to the ground and up. Ye shall find him and bring him to me alive!** It is only fitting that his youngest brother shall taketh his life from him."

Joshua needed to find a way to get word to Jacob. They needed his help. Somehow he had to find Jacob, and all he knew was that Jacob said he was going to find a certain maiden. There was nothing Joshua could do now other than search for Jacob, so he left out the front doors, looking back and seeing the backside of Isaiah and his gang marching to the cellar.

And then he ran.

CHAPTER

9

Jacob was searching high and low for this maiden that he had lusting eyes for. He stopped at a couple of taverns and had a few ales. He felt he deserved it for what he had just gone through with Sir Matthew. He couldn't figure it out, what had happened to Matthew—did he fall and hit his head? Because if he didn't look like Sir Matthew, then Jacob would not believe that it was him. He was acting so strangely, or could it just be his father dying was making him crazy, but then again, what was with his attire? Where did he find such hideous clothing? He felt heavyhearted for Sir Matthew and his father, but he also felt he deserved this ale, and nothing was going to stop him from drinking it. When he was done, he would go find Ms. Tiffany, and then he would find a way to get Sir Matthew out of the sanctuary and to his father for guidance before Sir Isaiah caught up with them.

"Good den, sirrah," the barmaid cheerfully spoke. "What'll ye have?" "Methinks I'll have a couple of ales," Jacob was cheerful back to her. "Dost thou knowest the time?" Jacob asked the barmaid.

"Nay I dost not. Ye might want to ask the lad over yonder."

So Jacob walked over to the lad to ask him for the time. He couldn't waste much time because he had to find the maiden Tiffany and then try to get Sir Matthew out of that sanctuary and to his father's deathbed.

"Good den, sirrah," Jacob said to this lad sitting at a table by himself having an ale. "Dost thou knowest the time"?

"Yea, it is none. I have cometh from the sanctuary and prayers hath ended."

"Thou wert at the sanctuary?" Jacob asked nervously.

"Yea, thither perhaps is trouble at the sanctuary," the lad stated.

Jacob was in shock, but he met the right person in time. He didn't know that this young lad was one of Isaiah's hooligans and this particular one loved to gloat and blow his horn and let everyone know who he was and who he worked for. So he gave Jacob all kinds of informative news that Jacob needed to hear so that he could act upon it.

"What be your name"? he asked Jacob. "My name is Jacob, and what be yours?"

"I am Honor Jonathan. I am one of many of Sir Isaiah's knights," He stated, proud as punch.

Then Jonathan asked Jacob to sit with him for drinks. He yelled over to the barmaid, "Wench! Beakers all around."

"Grammercy thou art most kind," Jacob said to Jonathan and sat down. He knew he had to drink up fast and get on with his plan, but he couldn't let on to Jonathan that he was helping Sir Matthew escape his deadly fate.

"We hath been looking for Sir Matthew for a fortnight. His brother, Sir Isaiah, is full of wroth, and he must find him and bring him to his father's deathbed. If he is not found before His Majesty dies, then Sir Matthew will be self-cursed. We must not let this happen," Jonathan said with earnest.

Well, Jacob knew that it wasn't His Majesty's deathbed they wanted to bring him to—it was his own. He also wasn't sure if Jonathan actually knew what was really happening. He did seem like he was worried about Sir Matthew not getting to his father in time. Although he still had to play along with Jonathan to get as much information as he could, so he sat with Jonathan for another fifteen or twenty minutes and then he had to make an excuse to leave.

"Perchance we wilts meet again. I have errands to run, and if I befall Sir Matthew, I will detain him for the king," Jacob said to Jonathan as he got up and left the tavern.

"Fare thee well, my goodman!" Jonathan yelled out to Jacob.

Jacob yelled back, "Adieu!"

Just then, Jacob saw Joshua running through the streets like a mad hatter. He knew something had gone wrong. So he ran after him, yelling his name. Joshua did not recognize Jacob's voice so he kept running, but Joshua had several years on Jacob, so he could not run as fast. Jacob finally caught up to him, grabbed the back of Joshua's tunic, and made him fumble. Down he went, with Jacob landing on top of him.

"Josh, it is I, Jacob, I am sorry I had to wrest ye, but ye wouldst not stay," Jacob said frantically.

"Oh, Jacob, what shouldst we do? Sir Isaiah and his hooligans art in the sanctuary looking for Sir Matthew. I sent the lads down to the corridors in the dungeon, but I did not tell them of the secret corridor. I pray they find it, Jacob!" Joshua almost wept as he told Jacob.

"Joshua, whither dost this corridor open too?"

"It is writ on the wall of the secret corridor that it shall end at the **window of the sunset**."

"What is the **window of the sunset**?" Jacob asked Joshua.

"I know not, Jacob. The monks and I have spoken of it many times, but we art not sure. We think the corridor ends back at the main entrance to the village, but I cannot be sure." Joshua said panicky.

"We must find out and get thither before they do," Jacob said.

They figured if they went to the main entrance and dug around, they would be able to find the exit of the tunnel. They had to do this without being spotted. They didn't know how many men Isaiah had on his side. As far as they knew, it could be all the guards at the top of the battlements.

They walked fast instead of ran so as not to arouse suspicion. They walked past a wenches' washing well. There were several women there. Some were mothers with their small children. They were washing clothes, and the clothes were hanging over several lines for drying. At that moment, Jacob had an idea.

"Joshua, methinks I have a thought. Those wenches over yonder—perchance we walk over and very carefully but apace pilfer some of their hanging garments," Jacob said with a sneaky look on his face.

"Have ye gone mad, Jacob? What doth ye want with wenches' garments?"

"We must find a way to get Sir Matthew out of the tunnel and over to see His Majesty Vincent. We steal the garments for Sir Matthew, so he canst dress as a wench. None wouldst have misdoubt that he is a she. Once we grab the garments, we run like mad hatters. Art ye with me or nay?"

"Aye, I am with ye. What say ye if we get caught?" Joshua asked. "Naught we wilts not get caught," smirked Jacob.

They started to head over to the washing well. There must have been fifteen or twenty wenches washing clothes and playing with the kids. This was a good thing, because they were making a lot of noise and the kids were laughing. With all the commotion the females were making, they might not even spot Jacob and Joshua. They played it nonchalantly and watched each other grab a piece of garment as they watched the women. Just then, Jacob spotted her. His heart started to flutter and the palms of his hands were sweaty. He just stood there staring at her.

It was Tiffany. He could not believe his eyes. There she was, standing under a tree, reading a parchment. She looked like an angel. She wore a full white trailing skirt that draped the lower part of her body. Her corset was made of white silk with specs of other colors in it. She had on a robe that was fastened around the waist with long bands attached to the sleeves near the wrists. She showed a degree of elegance while the harmonious outlines of her body were being displayed.

"Jacob, Jacob!" Joshua whispered a loud yell at him. "Wake up! What art ye doing?" He pushed him in the shoulder.

Jacob was in a trance but not for long, because Joshua smacked him upside the head after he couldn't get a response from him when he pushed his shoulder.

"Bloody hell!" Jacob yelled at Joshua.

"Pray tell, what that was for?" he still yelled at Joshua.

"Ye was in a trance. I had to wake ye up."

"Look over yonder. That is Tiffany, the maiden I was in search for," Jacob said quietly to Joshua.

"Jacob, anon, we must keep on track. Sir Matthew, remember!" Joshua almost scolded Jacob.

Just then Tiffany glanced over at the two men as she saw them quarrelling. She recognized Jacob and started to meander over to him.

"Dost not look!" Jacob said to Joshua with anxiety in his voice. "She cometh this way."

"Jacob, 'tis thee?" Tiffany yelled over at Jacob.

Jacob heard Tiffany call but did not look up. He started to kick dirt around the ground, pretending that he didn't hear her. He felt very uncomfortable, especially with Joshua standing at his side. He knew no matter what happened now, Joshua would have a story to tell his drinking buddies at Jacob's expense. Once again, she tried to get his attention. As she got within feet of him, he looked up and blushed, stuttering as he was finding words to speak.

"Tiff-Tiff-Tiffany," he said with surprise, as if he had just spotted her. "What art thou doing hither, Tiffany?"

"I might beseech ye the same, Jacob," She looked around at where they were standing. "Art ye washing thy laundry today or helping the wenches wash theirs?" she said with laughter.

"Oh nay, nay," Jacob said with embarrassment and looked at Joshua as if to help him out here.

"Joshua thinks he hath spotted a maiden friend but was mistaken," Jacob said while staring at Joshua.

"Thy three friends, whither art they?" "Oh, Lester and Frederick?"

"Yea, and what about Sir Matthew?"

"Ye must be mistaken. I hast not seen Sir Matthew since the last quarter moon," Jacob said with anxiety in his voice, hoping that she won't spot his lies.

"Jacob, ye cannot fool me. I spotted Sir Matthew when ye were playing in the field, covering him like an animal. What were ye thinking? The king's son, ye cannot disrespect him like this," Tiffany said with sincerity in her voice.

At this point, Joshua gave Jacob a nudge on his backside. Jacob turned to look at Joshua for help.

Whispering to Jacob, Joshua said, "Ye must tell her the truth. Perhaps she canst help us."

So Jacob turns back to Tiffany with the hopes that she could be trusted and was not on the wrong side of the law. He knew that if it were any other maiden, he would not speak the truth, but he had fallen hard for Tiffany and hoped that she felt the same.

"Tiffany, canst I put trust in thou? I am about to embark upon something that may well cost my life."

"Jacob, whither thou goest, I shall go," Tiffany quietly said to Jacob.

Jacob was astounded by what Tiffany just said to him. He now knew that she also had feelings for him. He felt so much stronger now knowing that he had more than one reason to get Sir Matthew to safety: he had to show Tiffany that he was a conqueror. But he still had to make sure that she was not a spy.

CHAPTER

10

"Guys, guys," Matt yelled, "we've been running now for fifteen or twenty minutes. Where are we going? Do either of you know?"

Matt was ghostly white by now and thoroughly dehydrated. He really needed to rest and rehydrate.

"Sir Matthew," Fredrick said, "we must go on, for Sir Isaiah and his troops may be on our tails as we speaketh. We must persist ahead of them. We wilts find thee a drink as quickly as we can. However, I beg of thee, keep moving on."

Just then, something appeared around the next bend. It was an outline of a shadow, and it was moving slowly toward them. Matthew, Fredrick and Lester froze instantly in their tracks. They clung on to each other, not knowing if this was the end and they were going to meet their creator. The closer the shadow got, the larger and beastlier it looked.

Lester whispered out loud, "Prithee, let this not be the closing stage. We would like to see another morrow!"

"What shall we do, men?" Frederick hysterically whispered back.

"We have to stand together guys, since we don't have any weapons, we have to attack this thing with our bodies. It's the only chance we have. Lester, you aim for its stomach with your head. Frederick, you aim for his ankles to knock him down, and I will aim for his head to knock him out," Matthew said frantically.

They both looked at Matthew as if he were nuts.

"It's our only chance! Unless you're cowards?" Matt whispered loudly.

"Cravens we art not!" Frederick said in a rage. "We wilts pounce on this creature or man, whatever it is."

"Then on the count of three, we charge at it. All in agreement?" Matt questioned.

"Yea," both Lester and Fredrick whispered.

Matt yelled out three as soon as he saw the claw poking out around the corner of the bend. They all charged at it, and within that second, both Lester and Fredrick yelled frantically at Matthew, "**Stop! It is Zerkin! Stop!**"

But it was too late. Zerkin put an immediate spell on Matthew to freeze him in his spot. Matthew was standing on one leg and the other in the air, in a running position, with his arm thrown back and ready to punch. His eyes were closed shut, and all of his teeth were showing. This was how he was posed in a frozen state.

Fredrick and Lester both told Zerkin to unfreeze him and that he was their friend, but Zerkin already knew who Matthew was. He was the one who guided him to this century. Zerkin looked Matthew up and down and circled him, sniffed Matt's feet, and then stood back and flipped up into the air and did a triple sommersault in the air and landed on his feet. Zerkin's eyes were a dazzling bright yellow as he stared at Matthew. Matthew slowly started to come out of the spell and fell to the floor.

"Matthew, art thou all right?" Lester asked.

"Ya, I think I'm okay. I feel a little light-headed. What just happened?"

"Methinks we hast better introduce you to Zerkin," Fredrick said. "He is the village wizard. We found him a goodly length in times past, outside the compound in the forest where the wooden gnomes live. He was found lying on the ground between some gnomes, having a nap. Methinks one of the witches hath put a spell on him, which is not an easy mission to do on a wizard. He doth not speaketh to us verily oft, so this leads us to trust that thither is a dark secret within him. He lives in the village with us and protects us from outsiders and evil."

Matthew stared at Zerkin with disbelief. "Zerkin!" Matt said, "You are the one that brought me here! I saw you at the trail at the campsite. You stole my mother's red watch and then led me to the castle. Why am I here, Zerkin?"

Both Fredrick and Lester looked at Matthew with bewilderment. They were confused and didn't understand what he was saying to Zerkin. Zerkin jumped up in the air, did his somersault routine, landed on his feet, looked at the boys, and whispered "***Follow me.***"

"Again?" Matthew said. "The last time I followed you, you got me into this mess."

Both Fredrick and Lester started to follow Zerkin, and Matthew didn't move. They looked back toward Matthew, and Lester said, "Come, Sir Matthew, we must follow Zerkin. He wilts show us the way."

"Are you kidding me? He's the one that got me in this mess!"

"I dost not know what thou art speaking of, but if thou art hither for a reason, then it must be important," Lester said with sincerity.

With that, Matthew pulled himself together and followed the trio. Matthew didn't have much energy left since he was very dehydrated. He could no longer run, so he walked as briskly as he could.

Zerkin was leading them through a maze of corridors. They had no idea where they were going to end up. Neither of the boys had ever been underground. The one thing they did know was that they had to get a huge distance between Isaiah and his goons and themselves, because it was not unlike Isaiah if he caught up with them to kill them on the spot. It would actually be the perfect murder plot for Isaiah because no one would ever know where they were. No one could hear screams from underground.

The disgusting odor was getting worse. Matthew had to cover his mouth and nose with his clothes to keep from smelling it. Fredrick and

Lester were starting to wretch also. Neither of the boys knew what was up ahead, but the stench was getting stronger and stronger. They weren't sure if they should proceed to follow Zerkin, and neither one of them wanted to speak because that would mean they had to let the foul air into their mouths. Just at that moment, there was a loud shriek, and it came from Lester. He grabbed his left arm and screamed. "Hellfire, lousy swine!" He had been shot with an arrow in his shoulder.

"Lester!" both Matthew and Fredrick yelled.

"Be strong. We must keep going apace," Fredrick said. "They art too close. By the devil's black hairy ass, we wilts get out alive!"

The arrow had been shot from a distance, so by the time it got to Lester's shoulder, it did not have much force left. The arrow stabbed Lester in the shoulder, puncturing the shoulder bone, and then fell out. His bleeding was at a minimum, but that did not slow them down. They were on a mission, and that was to get out of that dungeon of corridors. Lester picked the arrow up. This would be the only weapon they had to defend themselves with. They could hear from a distance the sounds of Isaiah and his goons approaching.

"How could they possibly be on our trail with all the choices of corridors to go through?" Matthew said.

"It is all by chance," Fredrick said.

"Zerkin, how much farther dost we have to go. They art getting closer, and Lester 'tis already hurt! And we art outworn!" Frederick yelled.

Zerkin whispered "**Dost not worrit. I am thy wizard, Zerkin. I shall protect thee and thy men.**" He pointed in the direction for them to escape. They were at an intersection with corridors steering off in each direction again. Zerkin had pointed to the one straight ahead. He jumped up into the air and did his three somersaults and landed on his feet and was gone.

"Where did he go, Fredrick?" Matthew asked.

"Zerkin wilts save us, my goodman, do not misdoubt him," Fredrick said to Matthew with nobility in his voice. "Matthew, thou looks pallid. How fare thee? Dost thee thinks thee canst make it a little longer?

And Lester halt thy yammering. We art hither to help Sir Matthew. I wilts bring thee both to the town leech when we art safe."

Fredrick felt all alone and responsible now for both Matthew and Lester, because they were hurt and sick, he did not feel that he had enough strength to help carry the both of them out. He was still counting on Lester to pull together.

"I'll be fine, Fredrick. Let's just get the hell out of here before they catch up to us!" Matthew cried out.

Lester pulled himself together and yelled, "Shyte. I might be outworn, but I will wrest the goons if it means life or death!"

As they started to run through the corridor straight ahead, Matthew mumbled under his breath. "I can't believe I have a brother that wants to kill me. What if this was Ben, what would I do?" As he looks down he notices that his mothers red watch is missing from his wrist again. He couldn't believe that once again the watch was lost, but he was too flustered with what was happening around him to give it much more thought.

"Fredrick 'tis so dank. We must move apace. Dost thou thinks Zerkin canst halt the goons?" Lester asked doubtfully.

"Aye, Zerkin wilts do what his powers allow him to do. Things art amiss, so we must help ourselves!" Fredrick yelled back.

The corridor they were told to go through was dark and cold. Once again they saw mice and rats running around squealing, and the stench was making it so difficult to breathe. They spotted some skeletal remains but didn't stop to examine if they belonged to a human or animal. All that was on their minds was to get the hell out of there and fast.

"'Tis a cesspool hither!" Lester yelled and gagged at the same time. Fredrick was running ahead, next was Matthew, and then Lester. "I see light, men!" Fredrick yelled out.

"Thank the heavens. 'Tis must be the way out!" Lester yelled back.

Matthew kept his mouth closed so that he didn't gag and just followed Fredrick. They heard some screams from off in the distance behind them. They hoped that Zerkin was taking care of business.

The corridor got extremely narrow all of a sudden, and with each step that they took, the walls around them started to crumble, bats were flying out from everywhere.

"What's going on here guys?" Matthew yelled out.

"Zerkin!" Lester yelled out. **"What have thee done?"**

"You think Zerkin has something to do with the walls falling in?" Matthew asked Lester. "Why would he try to save us and then do this?"

"Zerkin hath the wizard power, and quite oft, he is precise, but on occasion he hath a few misses," Lester said. "So we must move faster!"

"Look over yonder! The light, perchance this is the way out!" Fredrick yelled.

They got to the light, and what they saw put a huge discouragement on their plans and thoughts. The corridor had ended. They were now standing in a circular turret with no other way out, no way forward, and no way back because the tunnel had collapsed behind them. Just the three boys and the bright light.

"Up toward the sky!" Lester yelled. "There is an opening. I canst see the blue sky."

"Pray tell how ye thinks we shall climb these circular walls with no rope, Lester!" Fredrick yelled back at him.

"Methinks we shalt yell until another hears our screams," Lester said.

"No, there has to be another way. What if the enemy hears us? Then we are doomed," Matthew said.

"Sir Matthew is correct. We must find another way," Fredrick said.

So the three boys all sat down and stared at the hole in the ceiling of the turret to figure a way out.

CHAPTER

11

Zerkin

Zerkin had once belonged to the kings' family. He had lived for several hundred centuries, being passed down from one generation to the next to serve and to protect the family. Sometime before Fredrick and Lester found Zerkin in the woods of gnomes, Zerkin was the king's right-hand man. He knew of all the king's secrets and woes and was sworn to his privacy. Even if Zerkin was to be owned by another family, he could not disrespect his previous owner by telling the secrets that he was once sworn to. The king really could not have done as well a job as he had without Zerkin. Zerkin would tell the king in advance what the townspeople were doing, and if there was any trouble on the horizon. He would inform him of rioters, looters, rapists, murders, anything that could disrupt the kings' position, and he knew all this before it would happen. This was how the king was able to keep the peace for many centuries. Zerkin and the king had also become friends. The king did not treat Zerkin just like a servant but a close friend. Zerkin was passed on to King Vincent when he was put into the role of king by his father, although Zerkin had never had such a great friendship with any of the kings that he had served for like he did with King Vincent. With King Vincent, business was business and family was family, and Zerkin was part of his family. He grew up with him and, as a small boy, played with him. When he became king, Zerkin served him.

Zerkin also played with Sir Matthew and took the role of a third parent to him. Sir Matthew loved Zerkin, and Zerkin was very protective of Sir Matthew, for one day, he would be serving Sir Matthew when he became king.

* * * *

A few years after Sir Matthew was born, his mother, Her Highness Patricia died of tuberculosis. King Vincent was distraught. She was his only true love. He did not know how he would survive without her, and the thought of raising his son without her was devastating to him. King Vincent's health started to slowly deteriorate, and his mindset was lost. Nothing could take him out of his depression—not even his young son.

Sir Matthew was four years old when his mother passed away, and because of the depression that King Vincent was going through, the king's own mother and sister had to raise little Matthew. King Vincent spent time with his young son but had to throw himself hard into running the village to keep himself from going insane with the loss of his beautiful wife Queen Patricia. It was a mere six months later when he had met another.

Her name was Lady Juliann. Her husband Lord Chaldry had passed away two years before. He had contracted hepatitis and died very fast. She was on the prowl for another husband, one that was well-to-do. There was no way that she was going to spend the rest of her life taking care of herself, and she was rapidly running out of money that was left behind from her husband's family. She could no longer have maids and servants of any kind because she had nothing left to pay them with. She needed to find someone who had enough money to take care of her for the rest of her days and then some.

Lady Juliann was a very beautiful lady. No one could deny her that. She had long shimmering black hair that was pulled back from her face except for a few strands of ringlets flowing at the side of her face. Her eyes were large and brown, and her cheekbones were very pronounced. She had a very petite mouth and nose. All around, her facial features were of a porcelain doll. Any man would be proud to have her at his side to show her off, but she came from a family of thieves and murderers, and any man who had previously dated her had either come to his demise or vanished.

Lady Juliann was extremely lucky to find Lord Chaldry. He came from a family of prestige, wealth, and royalty from afar. He did not live long enough to find out the truth about his wife, for they had only been married for three years, and she had no complaints with him, nor he with her. He was able to keep her in all the jewels and expensive clothing that she desired, along with all the servants to whom she took all her anger and frustration out on so that she did not have to show that side of her character to her husband. If any of the servants had a complaint about her, they would dare not tell it to Lord Chaldry, for he would question his wife, and if that was to happen, the staff knew that they could become one of the wooden gnomes in the woods.

The staff knew of her family's past of evil wizardry of the worst kind. Her family was to blame for all the wooden gnomes in the forest. It was said that it was her great-aunt Emilia. She was an evil witch who would turn any male into a wooden gnome if he turned against her or any of her female family members. This power was passed on to all the women at birth, to every new generation and their offspring. Her great-aunt Emilia had put a spell on so many men that she decided to put her collection in the woods to scare off any men from crossing any of the women in her family.

* * * *

The woods were starting to look like a graveyard with all the wooden gnomes. The men would stay clear of the woods for fear of these gnomes. Others said it was a hoax, and they weren't real, that no one had that kind of power, yet no one would dare walk into the graveyard of wooden gnomes. There were also female gnomes. These were supposedly the women who sided with the men who crossed Aunt Emilia's family. It was said that the only way to free the wooden gnomes of their fate was to kill just one of the evil witches who cast a spell on any of the gnomes, and this would free them all. This was not an easy task, because the witches could sense when someone was nearby. Anyone with the intent of a kill would be spotted, and their minds would be read. There was no special mixing of potions or spells to cast onto them. It just took a common human being from another world with a virgin soul whom the witches had never laid eyes on before to do the job. This person had to have a clear mind, be determined and willing to risk their own life for others. Then and only then, the kill would be accomplished, and the gnomes would all be freed. It was not an easy task, though, to find someone like this.

* * * *

King Vincent met Lady Juliann at an outdoor jousting session. This was his first outing since his wife had passed away. His mother and sister suggested that he take some time to enjoy his village and not just rule it. Jousting had become a romanticized kind of combat because the knight could better show his individual skills and triumph as an individual before the ladies of the Court who were his judge. When all was over, the victorious knights received their reward from the lady of the tournament: usually a garland of flowers or more substantial prizes like war horses or, as in the romances, the love and hand of the ruler's daughter if there was one to be given. A feast was then held, at which the ladies as well as their champions were present, animated by the music of minstrels, and there were songs and tricks.

King Vincent had brought a few of his men along with him and was starting to feel a little more relaxed and looking forward to this outing.

He wasn't looking for anything more that day other than to have a good time as a spectator.

Lady Juliann had other plans for this day. This was the day that was going to change the rest of her life forever. She happened to be at the arena that day with her sisters Lady Bella and Lady Cassandra. When she had heard that the word on the streets was that King Vincent was searching for a new wife to mind his son, she decided that she would attend any and all of the outings that King Vincent would perhaps attend. She had been to many of the jousting tournaments and he had not attended.

Lady Juliann had spotted King Vincent, so she fled from her sisters and inconspicuously ran in his direction until she was within fifty feet of him. She was walking toward him very daintily, spotting a large rock ahead and decided that the moment was put right in front of her and this was going to be the beginning of a courtship. So she pretended to be looking in a different direction as he was coming toward her. Lady Juliann fell over the rock and into King Vincent's arms. Of course, King Vincent caught her before she completely landed on the ground.

"Oh, Lord! What have I done? Pray pardon me, King Vincent!" Lady Juliann said with shame in her voice.

"Art thee hurt?" King Vincent asked, alarmed.

Of course, Lady Juliann was pleased with herself that he was taking concern in her and that he now knew that she existed, which made this her big triumph for him.

"Ah, my lord, by your leave! 'Tis an accident!" As he was helping her back to her feet, she decided to take this moment to faint and have King Vincent feel obligated to help her. She went limp and fell backward, but not completely, with King Vincent catching her again.

He picked her up and carried her to the closest bench to lay her down on. There were many onlookers horrified. They assumed that she was truly hurt, and now a crowd started to form around them. King Vincent ordered his men to clear the way and give the lady some air. He took off his surcoat and placed it on top of her.

"Apace! Thou wilt bring water to this lady," King Vincent ordered to the first person he saw standing in front of him. With that, the man standing closest to him ran over to the well and fetched a mug of water for her and a cloth that he had found hanging over at the well. He ran back to the king.

"Your Majesty," the man said as he handed the water and cloth to the king. "Grammercy," the king replied.

He took the cloth and soaked it in the mug and wrung it out. He slowly dampened Lady Juliann's face and forehead. She was aware of what was going on around her, but she kept her eyes closed so as not to give away any suspicion. Lady Juliann decided to give the king a little more time to feel sorry for her.

"Men, bring her to the castle and giveth the lady a bed and fetch the town leech to see her," King Vincent said, and with that he stood up straight and headed back to his castle with his men. He did not want to make a spectacle of himself or Lady Juliann. He felt it was better to deal with her condition in private.

Inside, Lady Juliann was jumping with glee. Her plan had worked. She was being brought to the king's castle, and she was amazed how easy her plan turned out. Now her new plan had to involve a way to get King Vincent to fall into love and marry her so that she could become the new queen. She didn't really care if he fell in love with her or not. As long as he married her, she would bear a child for him, and that would keep her in his castle. That was good enough for her, because a child would not be a child forever, and she would be free once again to do as she wished. This was going to take a little more effort on her part.

The king's men had brought her to a room in the castle that was far away from everyone else. She hoped that King Vincent knew she had arrived, because she wanted to get started on her plan immediately. No time to waste. She was alone in the room for at least an hour when she decided to get out of bed and look around the room. It was stunning, the tall windows draped with red velvet striped cloth with gold edging—they draped along the floor like a train. The side table to the bed also had red velvet draping with a beautiful arrangement of fresh white lilies, baby's breath, and a dozen yellow roses. On that same table, beside the vase, was a picture of King Vincent's deceased wife, Queen Patricia, with their son, Matthew. She picked it up to examine.

It must have been taken shortly after Sir Matthew was born. He looked to be under one year old.

"He was a handsome little boy. Was," she muttered to herself.

Queen Patricia was the most beautiful woman that Lady Juliann had ever seen. She had dark flowing ringlets that hung over her shoulders, her face was like a china doll, with a tiny nose and mouth, her eyes were the color of chestnut. She had a sadness about her though. At that moment, Lady Juliann realized that there were a lot of facial similarities between the two of them. This might be her ticket in. She smiled immensely.

She carefully put the silver framed picture back in its place on the side table. She walked over to the closet and pulled the curtain back and was taken aback by all of Queen Patricia's clothes. They were still hanging in the closet. It looked like a shrine.

"No one hath cleaned out her belongings. 'Tis odd," she said, She continued to check out the rest of the room. In the bay of the window was an infant's cradle covered with white satin and pearls strung along the sides. There was lace draping from the top, covering the bassinet. Lady Juliann assumed that this was also left as a shrine after the queen passed away.

"Oh well." Lady Juliann laughed. "'Tis a sign from above. I am to be the next queen. Why else would King Vincent have me brought to his wife's room, and I wilts fill this bassinet up quickly for his highness!" She smirked and laughed as she walked away.

As she walked over to the bed and put herself back under the sheets, she heard commotion out in the hall. Then her door burst open, and it was King Vincent and three of his guards. He was yelling at them until he saw her, and then he calmed down.

"Thou shouldst leave now. Prithee. Nay one shouldst be in this room. This room belongeth to my queen. God bless my queen." King Vincent's voice cracked as he spoke, and then he quickly marched out of the room.

The guards graciously told Lady Juliann that she should get her belongings together and they would escort her back to the town square. She accepted their assistance courteously. As the door closed behind them she picked up her sachet and her cloak and looked around the room one more time, and that was when she had the idea to take something that belonged to Queen Patricia. It had to be something small that she could walk out with. Something that could be used to push her way back into King Vincent's life. So she searched the drawers of the armoire and in the third drawer she found a silver laced hanky with little red and blue hearts embroidered onto it.

"'Tis perfect." She put it into her sachet and left the room.

And this was how Lady Juliann pushed her way into King Vincent's life.

CHAPTER

12

"Come, Tiffany, we shalt explain in privacy," Jacob said to her as he took her by the elbow, Joshua followed, and they walked forty meters down through the meadows toward the woods where no one could eavesdrop on them.

After Jacob explained their crisis to Tiffany, there was a silent pause. He was not sure how she was going to react to this information. Hoping that she wasn't a spy, Jacob looked at Joshua for guidance, and Joshua looked back at him, shrugging his shoulders.

Then Tiffany laughed, and she laughed hysterically. Both boys were confused and didn't know what to think. They were getting a little nervous to say the least.

She finally caught her breath and said, "Jacob, dost ye think I am a spy? Thee both think I am a spy donst thee? This is why thee hast been so guarded."

Both boys shook their heads no and started to laugh also.

"Oh nay, Tiffany, we dost not think thou wert a spy. We hadst to be careful to make sure that thee was on the same side as the law," Jacob said with embarrassment.

"Oh, Jacob, thou makes me giggle, and I shalt not hold it against thee." And then, Tiffany recited a poem by Petrarch to Jacob.

> *I have offered you my heart a thousand times*
> *O my sweet warrior, only to make peace*
> *with your lovely eyes: but it does not please you*
> *with your noble mind, to stoop so low.*
> *And if some other lady has hope of it,*
> *she lives in powerless, deceiving hope:*
> *and it can never be what it was to me,*
> *since I too disdain what does not please you.*
> *Now if I banish it, and it does not find in you*
> *any aid in its unhappy exile, nor knows*
> *how to be alone, nor to go where others call to it,*
> *it might stray from its natural course:*
> *which would be a grave crime for both of us,*
> *and more for you, since it loves you more*

Jacob's heart fluttered as he heard Tiffany recite the poem.

"Lovely, Tiffany. That is verily beautiful," Jacob said in a whisper loud enough for her—but not Joshua—to hear as he quickly held her hand and then let go of it just as fast.

"Now we must get on with it. We must find the exit to the corridor that leads to the sanctuary."

* * * *

Fredrick, Lester, and Matthew were worn out and upset. They were enclosed in a tower with no way out but up. Yet there was no way to climb up without a rope. They sat on the ground, hard at thought, but no one came up with any ideas.

Matthew spoke up. "If only Zerkin was here. He was the one that got me into this mess, so he should be able to get us out, shouldn't he?" he asked both Fredrick and Lester. "I mean, he does have powers, doesn't he? Look what he has done so far."

"Ye has a point Sir Matthew," Fredrick said. "Zerkin has ye under his wing. He hast cometh to thy rescue when ye needest him so far. So why dost thou not call for Zerkin and see if he wilts cometh," Fredrick said with enthusiasm.

"Okay, and he has my watch again. I know he does. So maybe that means that he will come back for us. **Zerkin. Zerkin**, I need you to come back. We need you to come back!" Matthew yelled with hope. "**Zerkin**, we need your help. **Now! Please**."

They sat silently, waiting for Zerkin's appearance, but he did not come forward. Fredrick and Lester both looked at Matthew, waiting for him to speak up again. They noticed Matthew's expression in his face twist, and then they saw tears welling up in his eyes. Slowly, the tears started to flow down his cheeks. Matthew noticed the two boys watching him, so he quickly turned sideways away from them and wiped his face.

"Sir Matthew, no need for ye to shy away. We also art upset and want to get out of this dungeon. Ye must be broken with thy father on his deathbed, and ye art in this dungeon with nay way out," Lester said with a calm soothing voice and patting Matthew on his back.

"**ZERKIN, GET US OUT OF HERE NOW! I DEMAND YOU!**" Mathew screamed at the top of his lungs, with the tears streaming out of his eyes now. "**I WANT TO GO HOME! BACK TO MY REAL FAMILY! I WANT TO WAKE UP FROM THIS NIGHTMARE! I WANT TO PLAY WITH MY BROTHER, BEN. I WANT TO SPEND TIME WITH MY PARENTS CAMPING. I DON'T WANT TO BE HERE ANYMORE!**"

Both Frederick and Lester stared at Matthew with complete shock in their faces and their mouths hanging open. They did not know what to think. They thought that Matthew had now gone over the edge mentally. They both went over to Matthew and put their arms around him and tried to calm him down. The two boys, Lester and

Frederick, thought that maybe there was some truth to Sir Matthew's story of being from another time. Some things just did not add up with Matthew. He sure looked like Sir Matthew, and the voice was the same, but the personality and character was not Sir Matthew. Only Zerkin would know the truth.

"'Tis will work out for the best Sir Matthew," Frederick said reassuring, "Zerkin hath not let us down yet. He wilts cometh. Thee wilts see."

Then out of nowhere, there was a voice.

"It shall end at the window of the sunset. Look for the window at the northeast corner of the tower and push into the sunset."

"What are you talking about, Zerkin? The sunset would be up above in the opening of the tower! *Stop giving us riddles!* " Matthew shouted.

"Hush, Sir Matthew," Lester whispered. "Zerkin speaks in riddles. This is his way. We must listen to his way. Northeast of this tower wouldst be hither."

"Push into the sunset?" Frederick questioned. "What dost this mean?"

All three boys scraped the dust and particles off the cement walls looking for something, anything—an indentation, a crack, a hole, anything that would give them a clue. They were starting to get frantic. They knew that they were on to, something but what?

"*Look!* " Matthew yelled out. "There's a broken piece of wall here." He was tearing away the cement from this spot. He kept pulling debris off the wall until he spotted a rusted handle made of metal. "A handle. This is it, guys. This must be what Zerkin was talking about!" he yelled to the other two boys.

They all frantically pulled away at the wall to expose the handle and the trapdoor that was attached to it. The trapdoor was made of old wood with a rusted handle and had a skull made of ivory that was attached to the end of the handle. There was an inscription on the door that said **Window of the Sunset.** The trapdoor was three feet off the ground, and the door was four feet wide by four feet in height.

"This is it, men!" Lester yelled.

All three boys grabbed at the handle and pulled as hard as they could to open the trapdoor, but it would not move.

"Men, we must be doing this wrong. It will not budge," Lester said. They tried again and again to no avail. It just wouldn't move.

"Think!" Matthew said. "What did Zerkin say? '**Push into the sunset**.'"

Lester and Frederick looked at Matthew with a big smile on their faces, and all three of them used all of their strength to push the trapdoor open. As it slowly opened, the hinges gave off a very loud rusty squeak that had echoed off the tower walls. It was almost deafening.

"Stay, my goodmen," Frederick said with fear. "What if someone hears us?" "The heck with anyone else. Let's get the hell out of here," Matthew said. "Aye, let's go!" Frederick and Lester yelled.

With that, the three boys finished pushing the door open, climbed up and into the tunnel.

The tunnel was old, musty smelling, and it didn't look like anyone had used it in decades. There was nothing for light except for cracks in the walls where some sunlight had been able to filter through. The walls narrowed at certain spots where the tunnel would have a bend. Some of the rocks that made the walls were so large and jagged that they had to be careful not to bump into them or they could get seriously hurt.

"Oh, the smell! It is so rank," Matthew gasped.

"'Tis no different than the tunnel we used to get hither with the dead rats, Sir Matthew," Frederick reminded him.

"I wonder what this tunnel was used for. It is certain that it hath been closed up for a verily long time," Lester said.

"Hither," Frederick said to the boys. "Thither is an inscription on that stone." He pointed to a large stone ahead of them that had light filtering onto it from one of the cracks in the wall.

Matthew read it out loud.

> To those that hath entered these walls,
> Ye art close to the end of thy journey,
> ye Shalt not fear thy enemy is no longer near,

Close thine eyes, and breath a good breathe,
perchance ye should consider wherefore ye art hither,
And now ye can start anew,
Be free as a fowl
A life that wilts bring ye joy

"Wow, it sounds cool, but does it make sense? I mean the person that wrote that was probably a little out of their mind, huh? Be as free as a foul? What is that supposed to mean?" Matthew asked both boys.

"Fowl is a bird. To be free as a bird, Matthew. Methinks he is saying we hath another chance to start over anew and to make our wrongs right," Frederick said.

"Enow, my lads, we must go on. We canst leave naught to chance. Onward!" Lester demanded.

Frederick was taken aback with Lester taking the lead for once in his life. He had never seen his friend give an order before and never with a firm voice. Lester was more of a follower than a leader. At the same time, he was pleased to see his friend progressing in life.

They continued through the tunnel, coughing and sneezing at times and gasping for air at others. They thought the end would never come and they had no idea how long the tunnel would continue.

"Frederick, whither dost ye think this tunnel wilts end? Lester asked. "Me hopes at the gates of the village or in the fields of the meadows," Frederick said.

"So what happens when we get out of this tunnel to the other side? Hopefully in the meadows?" Matthew asked.

"We must deliver thee to His Majesty King Vincent! His Majesty hath beseeched for thee. My goodman Matthew, thine father is verily ill.

Perchance thou canst say thy good-byes to His Majesty and beseech his will for thee, and only then thou canst do as thee wishes. Methinks Zerkin hath put a fie on Isaiah and his loathsome pagans, so thee doth naught hath more worries. Sir Matthew, pray tell thine father we wish him adieu," Frederick said with a somber tone.

"Thank you, Frederick. I will, and when this is all done, can I go back home?" Matthew asked.

Both Lester and Frederick looked at each other in bewilderment, and then Lester whispered into Frederick's ear, "Methinks he is light-minded. The bump on his head must be seen by the town leech."

Frederick gave Lester an approval gesture, then they looked back at Matthew with smiles on their faces.

"Aye, Sir Matthew, that will be granted," Frederick said.

By now they had been in the tunnel for an hour, and they were getting tired and anxious. Then suddenly Lester heard a sound.

"Hark! Methinks thither is running water over yonder!" "What say you?" Frederick asked Lester.

"He's right. Look over there at the crack in the wall. There is water seeping through it. What does that mean, Frederick?" Matthew asked, worried.

"Excellent well. That doth saith we art close to the end of the tunnel," Frederick said with laughter.

"Really, we are almost out of here?" Matthew nearly shouted.

Both Matthew and Lester both clapped their hands quickly and laughed.

"Apace, methinks the river is nearby, if I am right—and methinks I am— then we shalt be at the end of the village verily soon."

With that, they started to all run through the tunnel, but they slowed down when they heard a voice. It was faint, but they heard it coming toward them.

"Shhhhh, guys, I hear someone talking, and its getting closer," Matthew whispered.

"Aye, I also hear it," Frederick whispered back. The voice was getting louder.

"Oh, methinks 'tis Rhymer Raymond," Lester said. "Who is Rhymer Raymond?" Matthew asked.

"Rhymer Raymond hath gotten his name because he speaketh in rhymes," Lester said.

"I recognize his voice. **Listen!** He speaketh in rhyme, and if he cometh toward us, then this must mean we art verily close to the end of the tunnel," Lester said excitedly.

"Rhymer Raymond 'tis a vagabond," Frederick whispered to Matthew. "What's a vagabond?" Matthew asked.

"A wanderer. Ye must know what that is," Frederick said as he tried to think of another word that Matthew would understand. "Homeless, without home."

"Oh, ya, we have some of those in our town too."

Rhymer Raymond was approaching them, his voice getting louder and louder as he rhymed his way toward them.

The horse wilts be the force
they wilts not prey on I
my strength is in mine eyes
for they wilts no longer be on course
mine horse wilts guide me home
for I canst no longer carry mine own
death is on my door
but i am not willing to go alone
the horse wilts be the force
they wilts not prey on I
my strength is in mine eyes
for they wilts no longer be on course
mine horse wilts guide me home
for I canst no longer carry mine own
death is on my door
but i am not willing to go alone
the horse wilts be the force
they wilts not prey on I
my strength is in mine eyes

And he repeated the verses over and over again as he walked past the boys, not even looking up at them, just kept his eyes glazed, to the ground, while reciting his rhymes as he kept walking.

Matthew noticed that Rhymer Raymond had dropped something on the floor. He wanted to see what it was, so he walked over to the item lying on the floor, making sure that the other two boys didn't see him picking it up. It was a pendant that must have fallen from Raymond's topcoat. It was a dragon made of silver. He decided that this would be something he could take back home with him to prove that this was not a dream that he was living. So he stuffed it into his pocket and returned to the other boys.

"What a strange person Rhymer Raymond is," Matthew said. "How can you have a decent conversation with this guy if he only speaks in rhymes?"

"Sir Matthew, no one hath spoketh to Rhymer Raymond since his accident. He wert a poppet when he had taken a fall from a blonk," Frederick said.

"What is a blonk?"

"A large horse," Frederick said.

"Oh, I'm sorry to hear that. Does that mean he is short a few marbles upstairs?" Matthew asked.

He got the strangest look from both Frederick and Lester. They just didn't know what to make of what Matthew said. Frederick and Lester looked at each other.

"What doth he mean by that Frederick?"

Matthew saw the look they were giving each other. So he knocked on his own head and said "Airling," which got them all laughing.

"Aye, well, Rymer Raymond is very teenful and difficult to look at," Lester said.

"Now enow! I dost not want to chide, but we must go on if we art to get Sir Matthew to the King! It must be getting nigh to vespers, and we wilts run out of daylight," Frederick said to the boys.

"Aye, ye art correct, Frederick," Lester said, we shall muster ourselves and continue on before we art outworn."

CHAPTER

13

It was late in the afternoon, and the sun was at its peak point, shining brightly in the sky. The birds were singing in harmony and soaring in synchronized flocks like children playing in the sky. It would have been the perfect day to lounge around under the sun and have some fun. Unfortunately, Jacob, Joshua, and Tiffany had other plans.

"'Tis hath turned out to be a wondrous day. I only wish we couldst enjoy it. Perchance when Sir Matthew and Frederick and Lester art safe we canst enjoy the rest of this day," Tiffany said to Jacob.

"Aye, I wouldst do aught if this day was not amiss, Ms. Tiffany, but then I might not have bumped into thee," Jacob said to her as he looked profoundly into her eyes.

The three of them didn't know it, but they were about to be joined with Matthew, Frederick, and Lester sooner than they thought.

They headed down the meadows toward the river. They were on the hunt for the secret passage that would help Matthew, Frederick, and Lester to safety.

"Dost thou wit a covert that we may seek the night? Methinks the darkness may fall upon us apace," Tiffany said.

Joshua spoke up. "Aye, methinks hence forward thither is a byre. We shouldst make it by nightfall. Jacob, dost thee bring the garments for Sir Matthew?"

Jacob spoke up "Aye. Methinks things art amiss."

"What say you?" Joshua asked.

"By my troth, I feel that we art encompassed by something or someone. I cannot explain but the perception is real," Jacob said with a frightful tone to his voice.

So the three started to look behind themselves, and in all four directions. Now feeling a little nervous that someone or something was following them. They all started to get the feeling that they were not alone. They could feel the hair on their arms lift and goose bumps starting to form.

"We must walk apace to the covert Joshua hath told us!" Jacob told them. "Josh, hath thee any weapons on thee?" Jacob asked.

"Aye," Joshua said as he pulled out a butcher knife from his boots. Jacob just shook his head.

"Worrit not, Jacob. My brothers hath taught me to fight. Ye wilts not be alone," Tiffany said proudly. She was a strong girl. She let them know that if there was any fighting involved, she had no problems jumping in when needed, that her brothers had taught her a thing or two of how to defend herself.

Then there was a rustling sound in the woods, with branches snapping. They started to walk faster and faster. Then fear took over and they started to run.

The night's sky had instantly turned jet black, and then there was a sudden burst of light in the sky in front of them, which jolted them to an immediate stop. It was a bolt of lightning, then two more, then three, then a complete sky of lightning bolts thrashing the ground with a crackling sound of flames right before their eyes. They were so frightened they didn't know what to do, so they huddled together, hoping by some miracle their lives would be spared. When it stopped, they looked up and saw a number of witches encircling them with the most wicked stares and scowls. The trio shook with terror. They had never seen one witch before, let alone an army of witches, and they hadn't even really believed in their existence.

The head witch, Bianca, spoke with an earsplitting echo in her voice, and the pitch was so harsh that Joshua's ear started to bleed. **"No harm wilts cometh to thee if ye bringeth me Sir Matthew,"** Bianca echoed.

If they did that one task, then they would be spared. The trio were shocked. What would those wicked witches want with Matthew? He was the king's son. No one can harm the king's son, and they had to have known that. The trio did not know that Matthew's half brother, Isaiah, was a nephew to Bianca, and it was essential for Matthew to die so that Isaiah could be in power as king.

Jacob, Joshua, and Tiffany played along and agreed to their demand. They did not have a choice, but they were going to warn Matthew and the kingdom.

"Ye must bring Sir Matthew to the woods of the gnomes by daybreak, or ye all shalt becometh a wooden gnome and live thine lives forever in my forest," Bianca wailed out.

Jacob, Tiffany, and Joshua were in complete shock.

"So 'tis true? The Forest of Wooden Gnomes is a fie!" Joshua gasped.

"'Tis not a fairy tale," Tiffany whispered as she stared into Jacob's eyes with fear.

In an instant, the witches had vanished, leaving the trio standing there in disbelief. They ran as fast as they could to the cow shed for safety, and then they could strategize their next move. There was no possible way they were going to deliver Matthew to the witches. They would risk their lives for his safety, but they had to make a plan and find him fast before the witches did.

They arrived at the cow shed and found large piles of hay that they were able to cuddle up in together and try to get some sleep, although they found it very difficult to close their eyes after what they had experienced.

"Jacob, I feel a little swoon. This cannot befall," Tiffany said deliriously. "And pray tell how canst we get to Sir Matthew before daybreak to warn him?"

"Ye dost look a little pallid Tiffany," Jacob said. "By my troth, we shalt find Sir Matthew before daybreak and deliver him to the king's castle, whither he shalt be safe, for not even a witch canst get through the walls of the castle, for it is as holy as the sanctuary," Jacob said proudly.

"We must all covert thither as well, if we art to leave the castle walls, we wilts becometh wooden gnomes," Joshua demanded, to which they all agreed on.

"Tiffany," Jacob said "I dost not want for thee to be entwined in this war! I fear for thee, although I am also verily happy that thee art with me."

"I too, Jacob, and the three of us together. We shalt be fine," Tiffany said with a encouraging smile to Jacob.

So they had decided that they would each take turns staying awake for a few hours during the night, just in case the witches returned. Once they felt each of them got a couple of hours of sleep, they would make their trek to find Sir Matthew. They had no idea of where to seek out Matthew, outside of the village gates, or over the bridge.

Joshua was the first to sit guard while Tiffany and Jacob slept for a few of hours, when he had woken up Jacob to change guard, Jacob told him that when the next two hours would go by that they would leave. Joshua agreed.

* * * *

It was time. Jacob woke up Tiffany and Joshua. Tiffany had hoped that it was all a dream.

"I'm afraid not, my love. We must leave apace," Jacob said.

As they stepped out of the cow shed, it was still dark. The sun had not even peeked from the horizon. This was exactly what they wanted. This way no one could spot them running through the fields. A few times, they had to stop so Joshua could rest for a short while. He complained to Jacob that he was not a young lad like him. He just needed to catch his breath.

They agreed and then carried on. Up ahead, they noticed the walls surrounding the village were getting closer. Jacob told them that they had to get over the bridge without the guards noticing them, or they would for sure think they were up to no good and then detain them, and they did not have one minute to spare.

They arrived at the gates, which were left open. Jacob and Joshua and Tiffany looked up in the sky to the parapets to see where the guards were standing ground. Tiffany could not see a guard. Neither could Joshua.

"Whither art the guards?" Jacob asked no one in particular. "We must remain quiet. Perhaps they art in converse with one another. Any rumpus, and we shalt be spotted. Extreme vigilance is a must."

Very slowly turning back every few moments to look up toward the parapets to make sure that they would not be caught, they snuck around the grounds close to the bridge where the trapdoor was to be.

"We must find this passage door," Jacob whispered.

"Whence we were at the sanctuary, we hath spoken of this passage door. 'Tis wert not far from the bridge. Thither wert a trapdoor underneath some undergrowth," Joshua said. "We must look everywhere. With almost certainty, this door hath not been used for many a yore, and we may n'er unearth it."

They were about to find out that Rhymer Raymond used it every day so it was not going to be that hard to find. They each took a different path and carefully, with soft movements, stirred the foliage with their hands and feet to find what looked like a trapdoor. If they could just find this door. Go through it, then the first half of the mission would be complete. Finding Sir Matthew was another challenge. They were hoping that Frederick and Lester had lead Matthew down the right path from the dungeon halls.

Joshua shouted out a whisper, "Methinks I hath found it!" Both Tiffany and Jacob came running to him.

"Grammarcy to the heavens," Jacob said as he looked up at the sky with his hands together.

Joshua was pushing the weeds and growth away from the door that was ajar.

"Someone hath been hither, but who?" Jacob questioned.

Joshua looked at Jacob with surprise and said, "And if 'tis wert Matthew, Lester, and Frederick? If they hath found their way out, whither would they be?"

"Me dost not think 'tis wert them," Jacob said. "Wherefore wouldst they leave the door ajar. They wouldst make sure to not leave Isaiah and his goons a sign."

"'Tis true," Joshua stated.

One at a time, all three climbed down through the trapdoor.

"Ye must be sure ye leave the door ajar, Josh. We couldst use a little light and air hither," Jacob said.

The smell was musty and it was dark. Jacob, Tiffany, and Joshua all held hands so they would not lose one another. The walls felt rough and jagged to the touch. They placed one hand on the walls to feel which way to go and the other clenched tightly with another.

Then they heard a sound.

CHAPTER

14

The walls were rigidly sharp, the halls were dark, damp, and swarming with spiders. The ground was laced with cockroaches and vermin. The smell was so pungent that it was difficult to take in a breath. You could smell death every step you took. They needed to move faster to get to the end of the tunnel or they would surely suffocate. They were dry heaving and coughing. It was difficult for the three boys because they couldn't see where they were going. They tried to stretch their eyes wide open with hopes that they could see something, but it was much too dark underground. Every step was not without their hands on the walls where parasites crawled over them and made them shudder with disgust. Frederick was up front with one hand on the wall and the other flailing in the air as if he were reaching for something, and Matthew had one hand on Frederick's shoulder and the other on the wall. Lester also had one hand on Matthew's shoulder and one hand on the wall to help guide their way through.

* * * *

Frederick was up front, Matthew in the middle, and Lester last. They reached a bend in the tunnel. It turned to the right. Frederick was a little sceptical about reaching his hand around a corner.

"Lester," Frederick whispered, "dost ye wish to be the leader?" "Not I. Ye does a fine job, ye doth."

The next step that Frederick took, he used his left hand to feel the air for a wall, instead he grabbed a face. With that, he shrieked, and Matthew and Lester screamed, not knowing what Frederick was screaming at. Then three other voices screamed. Hands were flailing in the air, trying to fend off intruders. Jacob and Frederick had slapped each other's faces.

"Who goes there?" Jacob yelled. "Jacob, is this ye?" Lester said with joy.

"Lester? Hast we finally found ye? And Sir Matthew, pray tell he is hither too," Jacob said with hesitation.

"Ya, I'm here, Jacob. Thank God you found us. We didn't know when we were going to get to the end," Matthew said with enthusiasm in his voice.

"Oh, my lad, ye have saved us," Frederick said with merriment.

"We must hurry and get out. Thither is trouble on the horizon. I will fill ye in wenst we get out to some fresh air," Jacob said with revulsion in his voice.

So they all grabbed on to one another and scurried out the tunnel, up the broken steps, and out the trapdoor.

They all took deep breaths. Matthew, Frederick, and Lester dropped and kissed the ground.

"We art alive, and we art free from Sir Isaiah." Lester was almost crying. "For now," Joshua said.

"We must get Sir Matthew to the king's castle. I wilts explain on the way. Hurry we must get thither before daybreak," Jacob yelled as they started to run.

They had to run over the bridge through the open gates as the castle sat on top of the hill inside the village walls. Luckily for them, the guards were still nowhere to be found.

* * * *

KING VINCENT HAS A REQUEST FOR MATTHEW

The six of them ran as fast as they could up the hill toward the castle. The crack of dawn was slowly appearing in the sky. They knew they must get on the other side of the castle doors if they want to save Matthew. They had the castle in sight and Matthew couldn't believe his eyes.

"Holy crap!" Matthew yelled. "Shhhhhhh," all five of them whispered.

"Ye must keep quiet, Sir Matthew, or we might be caught!" Jacob whispered. "But this castle it's so huge," Matthew whispered back.

They reached the wall that surrounded the castle. There was a knight standing guard at the iron gates.

"Who goes there?" the guard asked.

"It is Sir Matthew and friends," Jacob tensely spoke.

"Bring Sir Matthew up front so I can take a look at him," the guard spoke.

So Joshua and Frederick pushed Matthew up front so that the guard could get a good look at his face. He held the torch close to Matthew's face to identify him.

"Aye, ye may all enter. Sir Matthew," the guard said with sadness, "thee must go see thy father immediately, for he doth not have much time left. He hath been calling for thee for a fortnight. We wert aghast that something may befall His Majesty before thine arrival!" the knight said.

"Benjamin," the knight yelled, "cometh hither and take Sir Matthew and friends to see His Majesty and go in haste!" the knight said.

"Aye," Benjamin said back.

Benjamin ushered Matthew, Frederick, Lester, Joshua, Jacob, and Tiffany to follow him. They ran across the courtyard to the main door of the castle. When they reached the door to the bedroom where the king was in, they stopped.

"I bid you all to stay. Only Sir Matthew canst enter," Benjamin said to the other five.

"I can't go in there myself, guys! I've never met him before. I don't know what to say or how to act," Matthew said.

"Sir Matthew, by thy leave, thy father is waiting for thee. We art outworn with thy prating. His Majesty wilts not be hither much longer, and thee continues to deny thy father! Now go apace!" Jacob said with anger in his voice.

"Jacob!" Tiffany and Frederick both said at the same time with disbelief.

"Ye canst not speaketh this way to Sir Matthew. He dost not know what he saith," Tiffany said with distress in her voice.

Matthew was scared and upset because he did not ask for this. All he wanted was for a wish to come true. Not for his life to be turned upside down, and now someone is dying and thinks that he (Matthew) is his son. His head was spinning. He didn't know what to do. His new friends were pushing him to go in to see the king, and what if the king knew that he was not the real Matthew? What would he do then? They could have his head chopped off for being an imposter. Matthew shook his head and decided to make the entrance. "Just get it over with," he whispered to himself.

So he slowly opened the large wooden door, afraid of what was on the other side. The door creaked badly. He really wished some of his new friends could accompany him, but that was not going to happen.

The king was lying in his bed. No one else was in the room—for that Matthew was grateful.

"Come hither, my son," the king softly spoke, motioning with his hand for Matthew to come closer.

Matthew was hoping that with the king's illness. His eyesight would fail him so as to not be able to identify him. So Matthew walked slowly over to the king's bed.

The king was very frail. His hair was white as snow, and his face had a grayish tone. He wheezed as he spoke and was short of breath most of the time, and he used the last strength he had to speak with Matthew.

The king reached for Matthew's hand, and Matthew obliged and gave his hand to the king.

"Matthew," the king whispered, "I have one last request, and only thee canst fulfill this request."

"What is it?" Matthew asked.

Then the king went on telling Matthew that there was a dark secret within the walls of the castle, and only he and Zerkin and one other know of this secret. He went on to say, **"Several hundred years ago, a wizard by the name of Zollo had fallen in love with a witch. Her name was Bianca. To everyone's surprise, she was with child. The wizard would not take responsibility for this child. He did not even want to look at this child's face, for if he saw this child, then it would be just as well as saying that the child was real. Bianca was ostracized by all the wizards by allowing herself to be with child by a wizard. She was so hurt by the way Zollo felt toward her and the child that she took her anger out on the child. When the child was a year old, she cast a fie on him. He would never grow any larger and would not appear human. She would have rather killed the child, but the covenant of witches would not allow her to kill one of her own offspring. This child was part wizard and part witch. She did not believe anything good would come of this child. So once she cast the spell on this child she dropped him off at the sanctuary where he would be taken care of until a home was found for him.**

"The sanctuary had no choice but to take him. They could not turn away anyone or anything, and this was only a child. As the child grew older, he started to take on a strange shape. He looked more like a three-foot weasel on two legs, with a tail and a long snout. He was able to speak, but he did not speak much. He was quite intelligent and had special powers but never used them to harm anyone unless it was called for. He did not know who his parents were until one day when Bianca passed him by in the village and their eyes locked. They were able to read each other's

minds, and when he sensed that she was his mother, he flew in a rage and wanted to kill her for what she had done to him. She was afraid of him, not knowing what kind of powers he would have and disappeared, never to be seen by him again.

"One day, King Edward heard of this child and decided to take him into his home to the castle. This child was named Zerkin, and he has been the royalties' wizard for over a hundred years, passed down after each king's death. Zerkin has been an important part in the royal family's heritage and continues to be."

Matthew's jaw dropped when King Vincent told him this story.

The king continued, **"I am the last survivor who knows of Zerkin's doom. I had made a promise to him that before I leave to the next life, I would have the fie broken that was cast upon him. There is only one way that the fie can be broken, and that is for a young soul of the future to destroy Bianca. Only then can Zerkin become a normal wizard and look like you and me. But you have to be extremely careful. The witches can sense a fresh soul. They will know what you are capable of.**

"Thee art the young soul, Matthew. Thee must destroy Bianca," King Vincent said with genuineness in his voice.

"So you know that I'm not your real son Matthew?" he asked. "What gave it away?"

"Matthew, it is not by mischance that thee art here. Zerkin and I hadst this planned. Wenst thee wert at the castle casting thine wish, 'tis was the absolute time to bring thee hither."

"Where is your real son Matthew?" Matthew asked.

"Sir Matthew is in hiding within the castle, where no man canst find him. Not even his friends know his whereabouts."

"Do I really look identical to your son?" "Aye, ye dost."

"So all of Sir Matthew's friends outside this door really think that I am him?"

"Aye, they dost."

"Boy, I really didn't sign up for this, I'm only fourteen years old, I can't kill someone. What would my parents think? I could go to jail for this when I get back home." Matthew was shaking his head in uncertainty. "I really wish I could wake up from this dream. It's not that fun anymore."

"Hark," the king softly said, "in faith, none of this wilts matter to thee whence thee goes to thy world. No living man in thy world wilts know of this. 'Tis a secret this world wilts keep from thy world. Do not fret, my son," King Vincent tenderly spoke.

"How and where am I supposed to do this? I don't like the sight of blood."

"'Tis must befall by sunset. I am swoon and outworn. I cannot hold on to another day. Thee must tell thy friends outside to take thee to the chine at Bubble-Blore. Thee wilts see a cosh across the chine. Thee must go to this cosh and go inside whither thee wilts see a daggle-tail named Wilma. Thee must tell her that King Vincent hast sent thee to break the fie on Zerkin. She wilts help get thee to Bianca. The others must not follow thee. Thou wilt kill Bianca with no onlookers, or all wilts be for nothing," the king said with seriousness.

"Okay, but how do I kill her, and if she is a witch, then she will have powers. How do you know she won't kill me first?" Matthew said with a tremor in his voice. "Besides, my friends outside the door said they cannot leave the castle walls. The witches caught up with them in the field and told them to bring me to them by daybreak, and if they didn't, they would be turned into wooden gnomes."

"Perchance Bianca thinks thee art my son, Sir Matthew. 'Tis good— then she dost not expect a fresh soul from the future," the king said with excitement in his frail voice. "So go bring thy friends in to see me."

Matthew went to the large heavy door and slowly opened it as it squeaked once more.

"Come on in. The king wants to see all of you," Matthew told them.

They all looked at Matthew and then each other in unknown certainty of what he could possibly want them to come into his bedroom for.

The king held out his hand to them all. "Come hither."

"Matthew hath a task which needs help from thee," the king said with shallow breath.

King Vincent told them that Matthew was not the real Matthew. They were shocked to find this out—more shocked wondering how he looked so much like the real Matthew. It made sense to them though, because Matthew had been acting strange for the past two days, and he didn't talk like the rest of them.

He told them to have Benjamin show them the way to the underground tunnel that would take them under the village and to the entrance of the chine, which was still part of the underground tunnel. Once outside, he would see the cosh where Wilma resides. He told Matthew that once they reached the chine, he had to venture on his own to the cosh. The others could not risk being turned into wooden gnomes. As long as they stayed within the walls of the castle, they were safe. Once they ventured outside, they could be harmed, and no one or nothing could help them once Bianca had a tail on them. "She has to be destroyed," King Vincent told Matthew. "This is the only way that my people can live in contentment and without fear of Bianca and her witches."

He went on telling Matthew that when he reached Wilma, she would make up a potion and Matthew has to blow this potion of dust into Bianca's face. This would then paralyze her for several minutes. During that time, he had to kill her. He must make an incision on her wrist with a silver blade and then cut his finger and drip his blood onto hers. The mixing of Matthew's fresh virgin blood of hope would overpower hers. She should dry up like salt and spill to the floor.

Once this was done, the spells would be lifted for all. The other witches dare not take Bianca's place, for not knowing who will come after them. "Thus, we shall have peace in the village once again."

Matthew just stood there, as still as a statue, barely breathing until Jacob shook him.

"Matthew! By my troth, thy face 'tis pallid like the winter snow," Jacob said.

"Well, its just a lot to take in. I mean I have to do this on my own. What if something goes wrong. Will I ever get back home?" Matthew said with panic.

"Matthew, come hither" the king said as he grabbed Matthew's hands.

"Thy heart is young. Thy strength wilts help thee through this. Thee art a good lad, and thy love for thy family wilts get thee through this."

He pulled Matthew closer and said, "Matthew, thee wilts be ordained a knight whence Bianca is dead."

Now that got Matthew's spirits lifted. Now he was ready, and he felt proud that the king would give him such a task to perform. He felt if the king believed in him, then he had to believe in himself. This would make him a man. He turned around to the others with his head up high and his shoulders pushed back. "Okay, guys, the king has given us an order. We won't let him down."

Then Matthew looked back at the king and said, "I hope you and your son had a good life together, and I hope you can spend some more time with him."

"Thou art a good lad, Matthew. Hence, may God be with thee." He dropped Matthew's hand and let him get on with his journey.

CHAPTER

15

So the six of them, led by Benjamin, started on the trek to the underground passage where Matthew was to start his journey to kill Bianca.

It was a long, silent walk most of the way. Benjamin led the way, with Jacob and Tiffany behind, then Matthew and Joshua in the middle, and Frederick and Lester at the rear. There were whispers going on among the couples, but no actual talking. Matthew had an awful feeling inside his stomach and had never felt so alone in his life.

Joshua looked over at Matthew. He could see the fear in his face. He put his hand at the back of Matthew's shoulder and said, "Fear not, my young lad. This fear canst only eat you up from within. I bid you be strong. Thee art a warrior for the king!"

Well, that sparked up Matthew's face. "Ya, I am a warrior, aren't I? Didn't the king say that if I did this deed, then he would ordain me a knight?" Matthew asked.

Jacob and Tiffany instantly turned around and said, "Aye, he did indeed."

Fredrick spoke up, "Matthew, if thee is to be ordained a knight, then thee wilts be the youngest knight that we shalt know of."

"Aye," Lester said.

So they continued on with their walk and Matthew was starting to feel better about himself, especially with his friends pumping up his ego. They knew that would work wonders for him, and it did. They were even cracking a few jokes along the way.

Then Benjamin yelled, "Halt! Hence, Matthew, thee must go alone." He pulled something out of his pocket and handed it to Matthew.

Matthew took it and pulled it from its case.

"'Tis a spit-frog," Benjamin said. "This wilts cometh in good use if one needs it."

"A spit-frog," Matthew questioned. "It's just a small sword. Why do you guys always have funny or weird names for everything. It's just a m i n i a t u r e sword." He said the word slowly.

They all looked at Matthew and laughed. They knew he would never understand their English, and they never his, but they all got along so well. They all hugged him and wished him the best and promised after this deed was done, they would ask the king to help him get back home where he belonged. Lester and Frederick even had a few tears fall from their eyes. They both spotted each other and quickly wiped them away before anyone else noticed.

"Matthew," Benjamin spoke with importance. "Thee must not squiddle with a soul while thee art in the forest."

"Huh?" Matthew asked with eyes squinting.

"Dost not speaketh amongst the others. Time is of the essence," Jacob said to Matthew.

"Oh ya, sure, not to worry. I want to get this over and done with as fast as I can."

So Benjamin opened the wooden door that led to the forest and backed away from it to let Matthew through. Matthew had to crouch down to get through the door.

"Really? Was this door made for trolls?" The others laughed and waved at him.

Benjamin closed the door behind Matthew, and they all turned and walked back to the castle and would wait for Matthew's arrival back with the good news that he had killed Bianca. They could not leave the castle walls until she was dead for fear of her turning them into wooden gnomes.

* * * *

Matthew was cold from the dew in the air, and the sun was slowly cresting its head, but not enough to see where he was going in this unfamiliar forest. He could see the ravine and was told that the cottage would be on the other side. So he started to run as quietly as he could. He knew he must be closer to the ravine then he thought because he could hear himself splashing water with every step he took. The ground was very soggy. He spotted a bridge that went over the ravine, so he made a mad dash for it. Once he got over to the other side, he could barely make out, through the trees, a thatched roof over a cottage that was made of brick and knew that would be the old lady's place that he had to get too.

It was very quiet outside, not even birds where chirping, there was a slight breeze, and he could hear the leaves rustling from their branches. Wilma's cottage was charming and nestled among the trees so tightly that you would think no one lived out here. He ran from tree to tree and stopped behind each one and looked around to make sure no one was following him. He felt like a spy, and it was actually thrilling. His heart rate was beating something awful. He could feel his pulse pulsating through his chest. He was at the last tree before he got to her door and realized that no one told him if he should knock on her door or just go in. She was expecting him, but he was also polite and didn't want to invade her privacy.

So he ran from the last tree to her door and ducked down and knocked on the door.

He could hear feet scuffling about, and then the door slowly opened. There was no one standing face to face with her, and then she looked down.

"My dear lad, why art thee on the floor?" Wilma asked. "I didn't want anyone to see me."

"Cometh inside. Apace!" She grabbed Matthew's arm and pulled him in.

Wilma looked more like a witch. She had a long nose with an awful mole on the end with a couple of long white whiskers sticking out. She had thick white bushy eyebrows, pointed ears, and her face was very skeletal. There was nowhere on her face that did not have a wrinkle and a few more moles on her forehead. Her hair was silver with black streaks and just hung straight to her shoulders. She was a very ugly woman. Nonetheless, he was only going to be here for a short time and needed her help.

As he stepped inside, he immediately choked over the stench that was lingering in the air. He held his hands over his mouth, trying to be inconspicuous, and noticed that it was an unsightly little cottage made of brick and stone. The ceiling had open beams from one end to the other, the floor was made of red brick covered by dirt and straw, and the fireplace was so large you could walk into it. The dishes and pots and kitchen accessories just sat on open shelves, not like at his home where there were cupboards to hide everything in. She wasn't a very clean lady. He could tell because there were cobwebs on everything, even her dishes. There was an old cauldron sitting in the fireplace, over the flames. This would have been her stove.

She also had a tin bath in front of the fireplace. He was glad he didn't catch her while she was bathing.

"What are you cooking in there?" Matthew asked.

"'Tis the magic potion that ye wilts use to put Bianca in a daze," Wilma said.

"How exactly am I going to get close enough to do that?"

"Ye must stand in front of the witch and blow the dust onto her face." "What? How am I going to get that close to her without her killing me?"

"Thou wilt do it apace. Dost not waste time. Wenst ye finds her, ye must find a way to get close to her to blow the potion onto her face. Ye hast a fresh virgin soul naught from our world. Bianca wilts naught understand this. Dost naught let her misdoubt ye, or ye shall be cursed or mayhap killed."

"Well, if I pick a flower and put the potion into it and get her to smell the flower and then blow it into her face, that should work!" Matthew said with excitement.

"Verily, mayhap thee canst outwit Bianca. Wenst Bianca is under thy spell, thee must make a cut into thy finger and her wrist and spill thy blood onto hers to finish the curse," Wilma said with wrath.

Wilma continued stirring the cauldron while they spoke. She offered Matthew some soup, but he turned it down. The smell in her home was putrid it smelt like rotting feet. There was no way he could manage to swallow anything she fed him. He just looked around and waited until she was ready with the potion.

He then watched as she dropped the concoction into a vial with something that looked like tweezers and quietly said a rhyme that sounded more like a spell. Then she put a lid on it and shook it four times, it was sparkling purple in color.

"Take this, my young poppet, and becometh a soldier. Dost a good task and bring to us good tidings." She handed Matthew the vial.

As they both headed for the door, Matthew opened the door and she called out.

"Matthew, be watchful. Thine eyes must stay wide open, and be verily quiet like a mouse. Adieu Matthew adieu," Wilma said with trust in her voice.

Then Matthew realized that he didn't even know where he was to look to find her, so he turned around and said, "Wilma, no one told me which way to go or where I can find her."

"Yonder deeper into the forest ye wilts cometh across a fork in the path. Thither wilt be a sign. 'Tis wilt read **"Widdershins,"** The signage spins oft, 'tis knows whither ye wish to go. Ye must follow the path of the sign. Ye must have the flower in hand and ready."

* * * *

The breeze was starting to pick up, and there was a bitter chill in the air. The sun was starting to rise a little higher from the last time he saw it, but it was still not quite daylight out yet. He wanted to get this mission done fast so he could end this wish that turned into a nightmare.

"First things first," Matt said to himself, "I have to find a flower, one big enough and pretty enough, and then when I find her, I'll ask her to sniff it and tell me what it smells like since I'm allergic to flowers. God, I hope that works. I have to be convincing."

So he started looking high and low for the right flower. The landscape was similar to a storybook fairytale: rolling hills with wildflowers everywhere, small ravines and streams running into ponds with frogs and crickets making their sounds. Squirrels were chasing each other around trees and jumping from limb to limb. Turtles sat as couples, on floating driftwood in the ponds. Birds in flight were chasing each other in circles, as rabbits ran wild and deer munched on grass. Everything was so colourful. Brilliant green grass with coloured mushrooms protruded from the ground. He had never seen mushrooms that were red and green and blue with multitudes of colors on the heads. These mushrooms were gigantic. Some even stood taller than he did. The trees had funny shapes to them. Some were bent out of shape, and some had charming twists to them. There were butterflies of all colors and sizes flying about.

"Boy, all I need to see now is a unicorn," Matthew whispered to himself.

Then he spotted the fork in the path, and just like Wilma said there was a sign with an arrow pointing the direction, and it read, **"Widdershins."** When he stepped closer to the sign, it started to spin out of control. That made Matthew uneasy, like it knew who he was. Then it stopped and pointed to the east. Matthew waited a few minutes to see if it would move again, but it didn't, so he took that path.

This path was even more beautiful than the one that led him here. He felt like whistling and skipping his way through, but he didn't want anyone to see or hear him, so he kept it on the QT.

"I have to find a flower and soon. I don't want to be caught empty-handed if she finds me before I find her," he whispered to himself.

So he started to search high and low without moving much from where he stood.

"Wow, this is the most beautiful place that I have ever seen."

The sun was now rising higher in the sky. You could tell it was going to be a beautiful warm summer's day. Birds were singing over him and flying around him as if they wanted him to follow them. So he did. It was the most amazing thing. He walked with a flock of birds encircling him to a path that led underground, it was more like a partial tunnel. He could see the daylight one hundred feet away, but in this tunnel were the most beautiful flowers he had ever seen—every breed, every color, and every size. He was astonished.

"Wow, Mom would love this. It's like a greenhouse underground. How do these flowers survive under the ground like this?"

He walked through all the different trails of plants, smelling all of them, butterflies landing on his head and nose. Then he started to laugh. They were tickling him.

"If this is what heaven looks like, then I want in." If only he could spend all day there, but he was on a mission.

He spotted the most gorgeous of flowers he had ever encountered. It was a bird of paradise. How beautiful it was with its orange-and-yellow featherlike head with red-and-green beaklike resemblance. It reminded him of a parrot, but little did Matthew know that this flower did not have a smell to it. He put it to his nose.

"This doesn't smell. Maybe I can't smell flowers. Oh, but it's the perfect flower. I can sprinkle the dust onto the head of the flower, and it should coat all of it. I just better keep it away from my face."

So Matthew took the vial out of his pocket, opened the lid, and started to shake the purple glittery dust in among the orange and yellow feather-like heads. Amazingly, it coated the flower without color. No one would ever know he had covered it with a hex. He put the lid back on and put the vial back into his pocket. He held the flower by his side so that it would not be anywhere near his face. He looked around the enchanted garden one more time and wished he could stay a little longer, but the birds encircled him once again, leading him out from under the tunnel of beauty.

The birds were still singing, and the butterflies were flying up ahead going from flower to flower. He could see a cascading waterfall in the distance, glittering with a rainbow of colors as the sun shined onto its rushing water. It was an amazing sight. For a while, he had forgotten why he was there. He gave himself a smack on the forehead to get back to reality.

"I'd better be ready for this Bianca witch. Who knows where she will show up? Or if she will."

He saw a wooden bench carved into a tree, so he thought it wouldn't hurt anyone if he sat there for a while and just gazed at everything.

"Heck, I don't want to leave this place, and no one told me I couldn't sit down." So he sat on the tree bench and took all the beauty in. Like taking a deep breath, he wanted to hold it in for as long as he possibly could. He placed the flower beside him and just stared at everything.

There were sheep, white horses, wolves, coyotes, goats, and deer, all playing in the fields of lush green grass. All these animals seemed to get along with one another. He thought it was so cool to not have another human in sight, just these animals, like it was there planet. Some of them even came up to him and sniffed him and nudged his hand to pet their head. He must have played with them for twenty minutes until the animals froze where they stood.

Matt slowly got up from the ground. "What's going on? What are you guys looking at?" The animals started to make small whimpering sounds and ran off into the fields again and then off into the woods like they were going to hide.

The beautiful day was starting to look gloomy, the sky was getting darker and there was coldness in the air. He didn't like the sensation he was starting to feel on the back of his neck. "Something is up, and I don't think I'm going to like it."

CHAPTER

16

"THE KILL OF A WITCH"
Matthew's Encounter with Bianca

The sky was now pitch-black. The wind was strong. Leaves were blowing everywhere. He grabbed his flower and placed it in the inside of his belt so that it wouldn't fly away. if he lost this flower, then he might as well surrender, because nothing or nobody could help him now.

"I don't like this," his voice sang. "I have to remember to be brave. Wilma said I cannot let Bianca misdoubt me and to have my eyes wide open. That's what I'm doing." His voice sang again with worry.

It looked like nightfall already, and then there was a loud crackling sound. Lightning was coming from everywhere and hitting the ground. Not one missed the earth. Matthew fled to hide under the built-in bench in the tree where he would be somewhat covered. He checked to make sure his flower was still there, and it was.

Then he realized that with all the commotion of finding a way to get the hexed potion blown into Bianca's face, he never even thought about the fact that he had to cut into his finger and Bianca's wrist and bleed on to her blood. He hated the sight of blood. "Wilma never told me how long the potion would keep Bianca in a daze for either!"

Now Matthew was getting bewildered. He was not given the complete instructions as to how much time he had when she was under the spell. He was surely on his own now, but he remembered the king telling him that he was a soldier, and that if the deed was done, he would become anointed a knight. That definitely made him feel powerful and large.

"What am I going to cut through skin with? I don't have anything sharp." He looked around his surroundings for something that would work.

He then remembered the miniature sword that Benjamin gave him. He said it might come into good use. He pulled it from his boot and withdrew it from its case, and lo and behold, it was sharp and silver. "Thank you, heavens above, for answering one of my prayers."

Then he put it back into his boot so it wasn't spotted by Bianca or anyone else that he may have to use it on.

"Remember, keep my mind clear of all thoughts, just in case she can read my mind, and keep calm," he kept telling himself.

The lightning was coming in groups and faster. Two hitting the ground and then three more and then one huge one right in front of Matthew.

He jumped and was so scared that he almost peed his pants but quickly composed himself, for he knew this was a life or death situation. **And there she stood in front of him.**

It was no longer dark outside. Once she stood in front of him, the darkness lifted.

She was definitely a witch, Matthew thought to himself. She had long black hair with white streaks, and she wore a dark green velvet hat—kind of like a hoody, but it had a point on the end, and it was attached to her dark green cloak, very similar to witches' clothes in the fairytales that he read when he was a child. She had a wicked scowl on her face and just looked scary. She could shake any man, even a knight, out of his boots. She wore a pendant on a chain that had a star in the middle of a circle. Her eyebrows were freaky, and so were her eyes. Her eyebrows went from the top of her nose up into an arc over her eye's about two inches, her pupils were orange, and her eyelids and under her eyes were a black color. Her skin tone was ashen, and her teeth were yellow with black lips. She was quite grotesque looking.

"Well, and what do we have here," she said to Matthew as she looked deep into his eyes. Her voice was quite sharp, with an echo to it.

Matthew looked away from her. He didn't want her to try to take control of him or put him into some type of spell. He didn't know what she was capable of doing with her mind.

"My name is Matthew."

"Yes, I know that, but to what do I owe this pleasure to. You do realize that you are in my territory now do you not? Mr. Matthew?"

"Why do you talk differently than the others? You don't have that different accent like they do." Matthew questioned.

"Those simpletons. The villagers? Well, my dear Matthew, I can talk any way you would like me to talk. I have heard you speak with those boys in the village."

"You've seen me before?" Matthew was shocked.

"I know of everyone that enters the kingdom, mine and his." "By his, you mean King Vincent?"

"How is the old man doing? I hear he is on his last few breaths." She laughed with a sharp tone.

Matthew felt like slapping her but knew better.

"He is actually doing much better." Matthew lied to keep her fooled. This way, he could find out if she could read his mind.

She tried to look deep into his eyes again by bending her head forward and down to his level and leaning into him. He was very uncomfortable with that and he would not look at her.

"What are you doing?" Matthew questioned as he tried to back up away from her. "I don't like people in my face, and you are violating my space right now."

She looked at him with a twisted look. She wasn't sure what he meant. The words he chose, she had never heard them in a sentence like that before. So she backed away from him. She knew he was different but needed to find out how.

"So, my dear Matthew, why do you come here?" she said with a command.

"Why?" he didn't quite know what to say. "Well, I'm on holidays." After he said that, he realized that was dumb. He thought to himself, he'd better start acting like a knight instead of a kid.

"What is a holiday?"

"That's when you go away somewhere, somewhere away from your home." "And you are away from your home," Bianca said with a crafty tone in her voice. "But you already know that," Matthew said back with a snarky tone.

"You are very different from the other children, Mr. Matthew," Bianca said.

"That's because I am not a child," Matthew blurted out firmly.

"And a feisty one you are. I like the feisty ones—makes it much more fun." Bianca squealed with laughter.

"You're sick and twisted!" Matthew blurted out to her and then wished he wasn't so forthcoming.

"Do you know who I am, Mr. Matthew?"

"Not a clue, but I gather from when you said this was your territory, you must be some sort of owner of this land or caretaker?" Matthew said, trying to act naive.

"Caretaker?" her voice screeched once again with a loud echo that you could probably hear through the hills and neighbouring valleys.

"My dear boy, Matthew, my name is Bianca. I am the queen of the **Widdershins Territory.** You must ask for my approval to enter my kingdom! How did you find your way here?"

She was trying to put a scare into Matthew and threaten him to see if he would cower. She knew all along that he was the Matthew that she had demanded Jacob, Joshua, and Tiffany to bring to him. She just wanted to see how much fun she could have with him before she destroyed him.

"Oh, I did not know this, I was just out for a walk and came up to a sign that said Widdershins. It started to spin and then stopped, so I thought this was the way it wanted me to come."

Matthew knew that he had better get her to smell his flower sooner than later. He didn't trust her. He could tell she was going to try to get information from him, and the last thing he wanted was to end up being cooked in her cauldron.

She looked down at his belt and pointed to the flower with her long bony fingers and said "Where did you get that flower?" with anger in her voice.

"I just picked it somewhere along the way, I have never seen something as beautiful as this before."

"That flower belongs to me! You should have never picked it from the soil! I could have you turned into a wooden gnome for this!"

She was angry. Matthew couldn't understand why she would get so mad with him picking a flower. It must have some sort of meaning to her, and it did. When a bird of paradise is picked from her garden, it signifies the death of a witch.

"Give me that flower!" she yelled at Matthew.

He slowly took it out of his belt and was uneasy about giving it to her because this was going to be his only chance to get complete control of her.

"All I wanted to do was pick the most stunning flower I had ever seen and smell its wonderful aroma," Matt said with an innocence about him.

She looked at him with a twisted look in her face again and just couldn't figure him out. His brain waves were giving hers mixed signals. She just couldn't get into his head, which really annoyed her. She had thoughts of keeping him for a while to toy with.

He slowly handed her the flower, not willing to give it up. She grabbed the stem and said, "This **flower,** my dear boy, has **no** smell! It has **never** had a smell, and it will **never** have a smell. My potions have created this flower, and **you have picked one of my children out of the soil away from its home!**" she said very angrily.

"But it does have a mesmerizing smell! A magnificent one. That's why I wanted to keep it, if you put it right up to your nose and take in a deep breath, it is actually intoxicating," he said anxiously.

She couldn't quite understand Matthews's combination of words, but she was willing to believe him, because she couldn't read any negative thoughts from his mind and she had never met such a likeable boy before. Matthew was definitely a good actor because he was convincing.

It was intense watching her put the flower up to her nose slowly like it was in slow motion, his eyes glued to her every movement. Slowly the flower was raised to her face while she kept her eyes on him. Her dreadful orange eyes, which scared the daylights out of him. Closer and closer she lifted the flower to her nose. Then she took in a deep breath of Wilma's potion, at the same time, Matthew stretched onto his toes, leaned into her, and blew the flower and its dust crystals into her face. Her eyelids dropped, and she froze with the flower held to her nose.

"**Bianca?**" Matthew said. He wanted to make sure it worked before he moved an inch. He wanted to touch her to make sure she was actually under the spell, but he was afraid to touch her. She was just too dreadful looking and ghoulish.

There was no answer so he tiptoed around her, and she still did not move.

"It worked! Oh my gosh, it actually worked! Now I have to finish her off. This is really it. I really have to do this to save all these people and myself."

He took the miniature silver sword from his boot and stood in front of her and held it up. He backed up a couple of inches so he could run if she moved. He made a small incision into his forefinger and a droplet of blood had already seeped out of his finger. Carefully he lifted the cuff of her sleeve to make the cut in her wrist. He took several deep breaths.

"Okay it's now or never."

He reached his right hand over her wrist and slowly brought the sharp silver blade to her skin **when Bianca's eyes opened wide.**

CHAPTER

17

Matthew's jaw dropped, and his eyes burst open. His feet froze, but he wanted so badly to run far, far away from her. He was never this scared stiff before in his life.

He realized that she wasn't moving. Her eyes were wide open, staring straight into his, but nothing else moved. He finally got the strength he needed to move his feet, and so he slowly moved backward away from Bianca.

"She's not moving. She is still stunned. I don't know if this potion is working, but I'd better get out of here. I can't finish this. Not while she is looking at me. I just can't."

Matthew was so afraid that he turned around and ran back toward the castle as fast as he possibly could, hoping that he would find his way back. Daylight had come back, which was a bonus to him.

He ran back through the garden tunnel and out the other side, hoping that he would see the flock of birds to help guide him back, but to no avail, he was on his own. He looked back behind him to make sure he wasn't being followed, and he could see a fog settle in the distance and once again, it was moving from the ground up. It all started to look blurry to him, and he noticed a bunch of crows swarming around him. That really freaked him out. He kept rubbing his eyes hoping the blurry vision would go away. He felt like he was running in a tunnel.

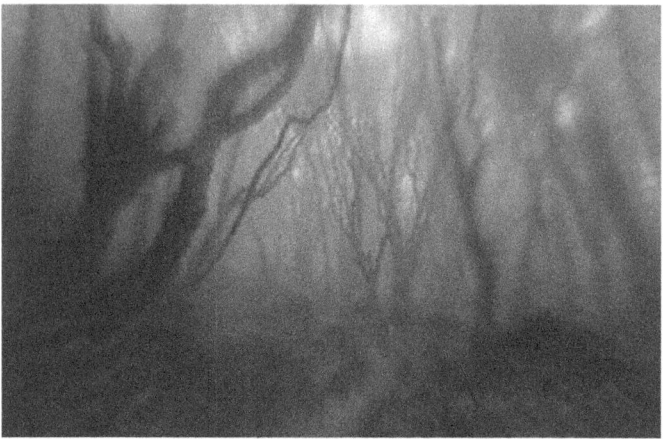

"What is going on with my eyes? Could the fog be doing this to my eyes?" he cried out to himself.

He turned his head again and started back on the run when he fell over a log.

"Ow, ow, ow!" he cried out, and then suddenly the crows disappeared. "I don't need anything to slow me down now."

He sat on the ground and rubbed his shin. He had splinters sticking into his pants, and he pulled them out. They had just barely broken his skin. His eyesight was back to normal. Must have been the fall that corrected it. He was lucky, because the fall could have enabled him to get to where he was heading to.

"Any more falls and I could be in real trouble!" he cried out. "I must keep my eyes wide open. I must be alert at all times," he kept saying to himself over and over. He stood up carefully and wanted to make sure he could balance his weight on both legs. He was fine.

"Okay, now I have to find that **Widdershins** sign again."

So he ran and ran and ran until he was out of breath. It felt like he had run a marathon. "I have to stop and take a breather," he said to himself. He slumped over and panted. He was sweating and thirsty. "I need a drink of water is what I really need," he said out of breath.

So he looked around for a stream to get a drink from. It must have been his lucky day because just yonder was a creek with fast-flowing water. He quickly ran over to it and bent down and scooped water into his hands and then into his mouth, dripping all over his tunic and getting his hair wet. He took an extra couple of scoops and threw it on his head and face. Then out of the corner of his eye, he spotted something moving from behind an extremely large willow tree. He took a few steps closer to see what it was. To his amazement, it was just an old peasant fishing.

I wonder if he can help me. He doesn't look threatening. Matthew slowly walked over to the peasant and was very careful on how he approached him, not knowing if he was trustworthy or not.

"Excuse me, sir," Matthew said with a formal voice. The old man looked over toward him but not at him.

"Come hither, young lad. Mine ears dost not hear wondrous well," the old man said.

So Matthew came closer to him and noticed that the old man was still not looking at him but more toward the tree.

"In truth, mine eyes dost not see wondrous well also."

"I'm looking to find my way back to the castle in the village, can you help me. I can't seem to find the sign called **Widdershins**," Matthew said.

"Whence comest thou?"

"From **Widdershins**," Matthew said.

"Ah, thou wilt not find this sign if thee is going to the king's castle. Thou canst only find **Widdershins** when thee is on the correct path. Young lad, thee dost not want to go to **Widdershins**. It brings bad tidings," the old man said with a somber pitch.

"I don't want to go there. I want to go to the king's castle. Can you please help me find the way?" Matthew was getting a little furious now because the old man was wasting valuable time by not listening to him. He started to get nervous and started to look around him to make sure there was no one else watching or waiting for him. He needed to find the **Widdershins** sign in order to go back the way he came.

"Nay, thee needest to find the sign 'tis called **Flesh-Spades**. 'Tis wilts bring ye back. I beseech thee to go apace, thither an **ug** with yee, and 'tis makes me aghast. Prithee, prithee, I fear for my life."

"But which way to **Flesh-Spades?**" Matthew nearly yelled.

The old man pointed his lengthy twisted boney finger in the direction behind himself and was jabbing the air with his finger as to tell Matthew to go this way.

"Thank you," Matthew said in relief and then he ran. *That darn old man. He cost me a lot of time there. I sure hope I'm still safe from her.*

He ran several hundred yards and then looked back and noticed the fog was starting to follow him. He knew he had to hurry and get back to the castle before it was too late.

"I bet Bianca is behind that fog following me. I wonder if she is still in the trance or if she's using her mind control to get me."

He ran as fast as he could, jumping over fallen trees that had blocked the path, running through twisting paths, and then he noticed up ahead a split in the path. When he approached the split, he looked around.

"Well, now which way am I suppose to go? He didn't tell me about this, and there is no sign." Matthew was very frustrated. He turned around behind him and saw the fog was not letting up. It was still on his path.

"I have to hurry or it may be too late, **Flesh-Spades,**" he said over and over again **"Flesh-Spades,** where are you?"

As he turned back toward the split in the path, there it was, the sign **Flesh- Spades** pointing in the direction he was to go.

"OMG, this place is so strange. How does this happen?" He started to run down the right path, and he could see the sun brightly trying to shine between the trees, almost like it was guiding him. Then he spotted a bridge up ahead.

"I sure hope that is the same bridge I took to come over here," Matthew said with exhaustion and panic.

"Oh, I think it is! I'm almost home free," he said with anticipation.

He made his way up over the boulders and rocks to the bridge and crossed it, running with nothing but the castle in his sights. He looked behind himself, and the fog was approaching him more rapidly. There was a thick blackness about it, and it felt very eerie.

"They're going to hate me back at the castle. I didn't get the job done. I really tried to kill her but I was just too freaked," Matthew blurted out while he was charging over the bridge. But he didn't care anymore. He just wanted to get safely to the castle and demand that they send him home. He had more than enough of this adventure.

He could see the castle very clearly now. The cellar door was not too far away, and he would then be safe. He looked back again, and the whole bridge was now engulfed in the thick black fog.

He got to the cellar door to the underground tunnel, and to his shock there was no door handle, knob, or anything to open the door with.

"What the heck! How am I supposed to get in?" He started to yell out everyone's name. "Frederick, Lester, Jacob! Please help me get back in. She's going to kill me! I need to find a way in. *Help!*"

He ran around the side to where the bridge and guard should be, hoping that the guard would still be there. Unfortunately, no one was standing guard, and the bridge was drawn up. Now Matthew was really starting to get terrified. He kept running and yelling his friend's names to help him. If he didn't get inside soon, the fog was going to swallow him up. His plan was to run the perimeter of the castle until he found a doorway in. He could see someone from the distance waving his arms as the bridge started to slowly lower for him to enter. He wasn't sure who it was, and he didn't care. He made a straight beeline for that person.

"Matthew, come hither. Apace, apace!" Jacob yelled.

Matthew was so happy to hear a familiar voice that he put all the steam he had left in himself and gunned for Jacob.

"Jacob, Jacob!" Matthew had his arm reached out and was about to leap toward Jacob's when suddenly it felt like the wind was knocked out of Matthew, and he was rotating up into the air like a spinning ball.

Jacob was yelling "MATTHEWWWWWWW, NOOOOOO. LET HIM GO! I DEMAND THEE, LET MATTHEW GO!"

The thick black fog scooped Matthew up and over the castle. He looked down and realized the fog was mimicking a large hand that he was sitting in. He could hear Jacob yelling for him. Matthew was so scared he didn't know what to do next. Was this a formation of Bianca? He figured it probably was, and that made him really nervous.

"I don't want any of this. I want to go home!" Matthew murmured under his breath in terror.

Then he felt himself landing softly on his butt, right on the rooftop. He looked around before he stood up, and to his shock, the fog was swirling around him like a spiral, and then it slowly floated away and there was only a tail of the spiral left. Right before his eyes, the tail of the fog exploded into sparkling debris of what simulated fireworks. Once the fog had passed, Zerkin was standing there, staring at him.

CHAPTER

18

"ZERKIN?" Matthew yelled. "That fog was **YOU!** Why didn't you show yourself earlier instead of freaking me out all that time? I thought I was a goner!" Matthew said furiously.

"Prithee, I bid you do not chide me. I was only to see you back safely," Zerkin spoke timidly.

"That's the most I've heard you speak since I laid eyes upon you," Matthew said delicately. "So you followed me back here all the way to make sure I got back safely? I thank you for that, but you should have let me know it was you. I thought it was Bianca following me."

At that moment, everyone appeared on the rooftop: Jacob, Joshua, Tiffany, Lester, Fredrick, and Benjamin. They all ran up to Matthew, hugging him, telling him how proud they were of what he had tried to do.

"But I didn't kill her. I was not able to fulfill my duty," Mathew sadly spoke.

"Naught to worrit, Matthew. Where have thee the spit-frog?" Benjamin asked.

"The small sword you gave me? I don't know what happened to it. I was just about to cut into her wrist when she was under the spell that Wilma made, when her eyes suddenly opened, and that's when I ran. I'm so sorry I did not accomplish my deed," Matthew said with a heavy heart.

"Perchance thither is another way," Benjamin said. "Stay, I shalt be back. Ye must all keep out an eye for Bianca. 'Tis wilts not be long for she wilts find us. The curse must be worn off." Benjamin yelled as he ran back into the castle to fetch a weapon.

They all huddled together in a group until Benjamin arrived back. They didn't know what his plan was, but they were nervous up there in the open sky where they could be spotted by any witch who might come along.

"Dost not be worrit. I wilts fend Bianca off. She wilts not hurt my friends. I wilts put my life in front of ye all," Zerkin said proudly.

No one wanted to see Zerkin or anyone else get hurt. The job just needed to get done. She had to die, and as nervous as they all were, they were also anxious to get it over with so they did not have to look over their shoulders anymore.

It seemed like Benjamin was taking forever to get back, but he was only gone for fifteen minutes when he came bursting through the door with a silver arrow and a bow in his hands. He ran up to Matthew and handed him the bow and arrow.

Matthew had a dazed look upon him.

"What the heck is this for?" Matthew shrieked as he accepted the bow and arrow.

"Ye must be the one, Matthew, to destroy Bianca. It canst only be thee, and the silver arrow must go straight into her heart. 'Tis the only way for her to die now. Thou canst not get close enough to spill thy blood onto hers, so thee must make the kill through the heart." Benjamin said earnestly.

"Thou shouldst hide over yonder nearest the postern, and wenst she cometh, she wilt see only us. Ye must take her on surprise, Matthew!"

Benjamin shouted at him. "Matthew! Art ye listening to me?" Benjamin was trying to yell over the sound of the harsh wind.

The others came closer to Matt and reassured him that he was going to do well and that they could all count on him to do the job. He was starting to realize the depth that he was into at this stage. He had to take another's life. He was still hoping that when this was all over it would only be a dream. He shook his head back and forth and then loosened his hands and arms by shaking them around in circles.

"I am so nervous and tense," Matthew said, so Tiffany came up behind him and started to massage his neck and shoulders. He really liked that and felt he could stay there a little longer while she did that.

"**ENOW**!" Benjamin yelled. "Methinks Bianca is hither!"

Matthew quickly ran over to the postern and hid the best he could. He would wait until he had an absolute perfect shot of her and then go for it. There were no margins for errors. He had one arrow and one chance. He had to make it work. The postern that Matt hid near was up a small flight of stairs on top of the roof. It had its own crowned top with parapets, and he was able to hide beneath the parapets and yet be up higher than the rest of his friends so he could get a better aim.

Benjamin and Zerkin were standing in the open, just staring at the sky. Frederick and Lester were cowering in a corner of the roof, hugging each other and trying to peek through each other's armpits to see Bianca. Joshua, Jacob, and Tiffany were hiding behind an old broken-down cannon. The section of roof they were on was quite an open space, not much to hide under or behind. So they just hoped that Matt would get that opportunity to kill her before she did them in.

Bianca arrived with a tail of flame shooting out of the end of her broom. She flew in circles around the rooftop, looking down toward them. She did several swoops inside the parapet walls and got very close to them at times. She was very angry. They could see the fireballs in her eyes.

Then her voice echoed in a very harsh rasp.

"**Whither is Matthew? I demand ye tells me!**" she shrieked.

No one said anything. They were all too afraid to be the first one to speak, and no one looked up at Matthew because they didn't want Bianca to spot him before he got a chance to aim.

Her voice was now wailing, and the sound was so sharp and ear-piercing that they had to cover their ears when she spoke because it was so painful.

"Cravens ye all art! Yee wilts all pay for what thy friend has done! Matthew durst to put a spell on me. He wilts pay with his pathetic life as ye all wilts with thine!"

She continued to fly around, shooting flames out and hitting anything and anyone she could get.

The six of them ran from one spot to another to hide without getting hit by the fireballs. Horrible commotion was going on between them, screams and cries, and anger toward Bianca.

Then Tiffany yelled out at Bianca. **"Wherefore canst Thou not fight fair like a human, instead of a witch!"** she yelled in anger at Bianca.

Jacob quickly grabbed Tiffany and put his hand on her mouth.

"Dost ye wants to be killed, Tiffany? 'tis wilts happen if ye dost naught keep silent!" Jacob said in fury to her.

Bianca sent a fireball aiming it at Tiffany, but with luck, she and Jacob got out of the way in time.

Then the sky went pitch-black with no stars in sight. There were literally hundreds of red-and-orange eyes in the sky with flames around the eyes. It looked like a firestorm of eyes all looking down at them. Sparks of fire were shooting out from the sky. The eyes all looked so deathly fierce.

Everyone was shocked at what they saw, and they were shaking with fear and hoped this night would end soon.

Matthew could not believe what he was witnessing, yet he could see something the others couldn't. He saw Bianca in the midst of all the eyes, sitting on her broom, and it seemed like she was looking straight at him. Yet she wasn't making a move for him. Was he shielded by something that she could not see through? He wasn't sure but he wasn't going to wait any longer. Now was the time. He aimed his bow, placed the silver pointed arrow onto the arrow rest. He took a deep breath, looked through the sight window, pulled back on the bowstring as far as he possible could. He made sure he would have a direct shot at her heart, and then he let go of the arrow.

It seemed like the arrow was flying in slow motion. It took forever to get to her. Everyone below had watched the arrow flying through the air, but they didn't know what Matthew was shooting at because they could not see Bianca. They thought that Matthew was just shooting at the sky.

They were all upset at the sight of this because they knew it was their only chance.

As they all stood there with mouths hanging open or hands over their mouths, they heard Matthew yelling at top of his lungs. **"Take that, you old battle axe!"**

The silver arrow made it to her heart and went directly through to the other side. It was a perfect hit. The screams that came from the skies were horrendous.

The eyes in the sky started to fade away until there was nothing left but Bianca, just perched on her broom. She started to disintegrate, starting from her feet and slowly up to her chest as the silver arrow fell out of the sky and landed on the rooftop of the castle. Then she was gone.

The dark night was full of luminous dazzling stars again. Then the sound of cheers and clapping and yelling was filling the air.

Matthew's heart was pounding so hard. He could not believe he actually hit the target and that it was over and done, finished, no more. He could finally go home. He grabbed his bow and ran down the stairs to the lower level where everyone came out running toward him and hugging him. Benjamin and Joshua grabbed Matthew and threw him up between them, onto their shoulders, and pranced around the roof chanting, "We wilts honor thee, Matthew, hence, for thee hast saved the village. Thee wilts be ordained a knight and be named Sir Matthew, knight who hath ended the war of the witches!" Benjamin yelled with excitement.

Benjamin and Joshua placed Matt back onto the ground as they heard Tiffany and Jacob yell for them to come and look at what they have found. At the exact spot where the silver arrow landed there was a pile of ashen dust. This was Bianca's remains. Benjamin picked up the sword and gave it to Matt.

"Thou shalt taketh this sword, and it shalt bring luck to thee hence." Benjamin said to Matt.

"I ask thee. What dost thee with this hellish ash of Bianca?" Lester asked Benjamin.

Just then, Zerkin walked out of hiding and walked over to the ashes of his mother. He had a satchel with him and began filling it with his mother's ashes.

"Zerkin what are you going to do with the ashes?" Matthew asked.
"Me puts it with the others. Makes good fertilizer," Zerkin said.

"Zerkin, wherefore hast this fie on ye not been broken? Ye is still a creature." Lester asked with curiosity.

"Ah, naught to worrit over, my good lad. For the fie to be broken, I must consume a morsel of me mother's ash," Zerkin explained.

Everyone cringed at the thought of what Zerkin had to do, but if it broke the curse, then so be it.

After Zerkin collected all of the ash, he walked over to a corner of the roof and sat down facing the stone wall. He opened the satchel and picked up a handful of ash. He held it up to the heavens and shouted in a fuming mode. **"I hath been without father and mother my whole being. Ye fied me because ye did not like thyself or my father. I was once a mortal soul until ye couldst not stand the sight of thyself. Hence forward ye shall burn in eternal hell for what ye hast done to the village people and thy only heir.**

> **Thee walks this darkened night alone**
> **No tear will shed**
> **For now thee is dead**
> **The sun wilts shine more oft**
> **And the village yells Huzzah!**

We shall dance, we shall sing,
And we shall drink
And for Thee thither shall n'er be a morrow
As I swallow this forsaken ash,
May the devil taketh
this fie and it shalt die with thee.

And with that, Zerkin swallowed a little of his mother's ashes. The others stood there in awe and watched Zerkin transform from a doglike creature into a genuine human being. They could not believe what was transpiring right in front of their eyes. He was a tall, stunning young man—a tall, stunning, naked young man. When he realized that he wasn't wearing any clothing, he hurriedly covered his privates with his hands. Benjamin took off his topcoat and gave it to Zerkin to cover himself with.

"My goodman," Jacob said, "ye is a stunning specimen of a man, and I am of great certainty maiden Tiffany dost think alike."

Tiffany bowed her head in embarrassment, with a large grin on her face for what had just been bared to her eyes, but she also approved, he was a fetching young man.

After everyone congratulated Zerkin for his new beginnings and Matthew for his triumph, they all went back into the castle to rejoice.

"We have to tell the king of the great news. Now he can live the rest of his life in peace, and his promise to Zerkin has been fulfilled!" Matthew said with passion.

"Aye," Jacob and Benjamin said.

"Let us go to His Majesty and bestow him the greatest of news," Jacob also replied.

So they all merrily walked toward the king's bedroom, and there standing outside the king's bedroom were two guards.

"We cometh to give His Majesty the greatest of tidings," Benjamin said to the guards.

"His Majesty hath passed" the guard said somberly.

They all bowed their heads down, and a few tears were shed. They wanted to see the king's face as they told him that Bianca was dead. Now he was gone and would never know that Zerkin was at last free of the curse.

The guard spoke up and said "'Tis this Matthew?" pointing to Matt. "Yes," Matthew spoke up.

"Thither wilts be a celebration in thy honour and thee wilts be ordained a knight, as requested from the king."

"So the king knew that I killed Bianca?" Matthew asked.

"Aye, 'tis was shortly anon His Majesty hath saith thou canst go home." **"I can go home! Really!"**

The smile on Matthews face stretched from ear to ear. He was so thrilled that this was at last coming to an end, and he could finally get back to reality.

They all patted Matthew on the back and were escorted to the festivity room where Matthew would be appointed a knight and then a feast was to be had by all with music and drink. A well-deserved and fine time they would all have. Indeed.

CHAPTER

19

"My Goodman Matthew, I shall be forever in thy debt. Thou wert so brave for what thee hath done for me. No other man couldst," Zerkin said proudly to Matthew as he had his hands on Matthews's shoulders.

"Oh, don't mention it. Anyone else in my shoes would have done the same thing. I think."

Zerkin took the silver arrow that Matthew used to kill Bianca with and slid his hands over the end of the tip of it, blew on it, and then said to the arrow:

"Whither thou goest, I shall go."

And then he gave it to Matthew. As Matthew put his hands out to receive it, Zerkin replied.

"If thou art ever in needest for mine help, taketh this arrow and place thy hand on the silver end and call my name. I shall be thither. This I promise thee, Matthew," Zerkin said truthfully.

"Wow! Thanks, Zerkin, I will never forget this journey or any of you. I am actually going to miss all of you. If the circumstances were different, I would love to hang out with you guys." Matthew said with a smile.

"What is *hang out*?" Lester questioned Matthew.

"Oh, never mind. It's just a term we use in the future." Matthew laughed.

"Excellent well! Perchance we will meet then," Jacob said. "But methinks we shouldst allow Matthew on his way home."

"Before I do go, I have been meaning to ask what happened to Isaiah and his goons. And now that the king is dead, who will be in charge here?" Matthew questioned.

"Isaiah and his goons art naught but horse manure. They did not die in vain. They shall be used for fertilizer for the crops." Zerkin said with satisfaction.

"Former Queen Juliann," Jacob said, "she hath been ostracized and banned from the castle. She no longer is addressed queen. She hath gone into hiding. She durst cometh out of hiding and wenst she doth we shall wrest her." Jacob furiously stated.

"As for our dear departed king, may he rest in peace," Zerkin said as they all bowed their heads in silence for a moment. "The reign of king shall go to Sir Matthew, his heir," Zerkin said as he looked and smiled at Matthew and said "not the future Matthew" with a smile.

"Oh that's great news. I just wish I was able to meet the real Sir Matthew, and I'm so happy that I was able to help. Maybe this will change the outcome of the future for you all. I hope for good things to come," Matthew said with a smile.

With that, they all walked merrily out of the castle together. Matthew, Jacob, Tiffany, Joshua, Lester, Frederick, Zerkin, and Benjamin. As they walked through the meadows and up over the rolling hills to the spot where the boys originally found Matthew, they laughed and joked, and even a few tears were shed.

It was a beautiful day. The sun was shining, and the birds were singing. There were people in the fields with their children playing, men and women walking hand in hand, women picking flowers with their baskets, dogs running wild, and sheep and horses wandering around the grounds. As Matthew looked around at everything that was going on around him, he realized that after all he had just gone through, this was really a beautiful and peaceful place to live, and just for a moment, he wished that he did not have to go back home.

They reached the rock where Matthew was first discovered.

Lester walked up to Matthew and put his arm around his shoulder and said, "My dear Matthew, perhaps one day I wilts make it to thy world, and then thee canst show me this Wii." He laughed as he patted his back.

"You betcha, Les." Matthew smirked.

Lester looked at Matthew and said, "I rather like Les. Grammercy." Lester looked at his friends and said, "Ye canst call me Les from this moment on!"

Then Frederick and Benjamin came up to Matthew. They each gave him a hug and Frederick said, "I wilts ne'r forget thee, my good friend."

And then Benjamin also said, "I shall think of thee oft."

Joshua was next. He shook Matthew's hand and said, "Ye art a good man, Matthew, and methinks ye might want thy attire to dress in." So he handed him his clothes and his knapsack.

Matthew took his items and went behind the rock to put his own clothes on. He took the silver dragon pendant that Rymer Raymond dropped out of the pocket of his borrowed clothes and placed it into his knapsack and gave back Joshua the clothes they lent him. When he came out from behind the rock, Jacob and Tiffany were there to say their good-byes next, and Tiffany started to laugh when she saw how he was dressed. She covered her mouth, and then said, "Oh, Matthew, I bid thee, pray pardon me. Who is this **S p i d e r m a n?**" she slowly pronounced out.

Matthew looked down at his shirt and said, "Oh, Spiderman. He is a great American hero."

With that they all say, "Ahhh."

She walked over and kissed him on the lips and then slowly walked backward. His face went several shades of red as everyone started to laugh.

"Hath ye ne'r been kissed by a maiden ere, Matthew?" Jacob asked. "Nay," Matthew said, embarrassed. And then they all laughed in hysterics.

"Matthew, I shall verily miss thee. We may ne'r see thee again. Mayhap in the next life. Grammercy for thy bravery," Jacob said as he gave Matthew a giant hug.

Zerkin was the last to say his good-byes, but he was to walk Matthew to the spot of no return. Before they left, Matthew addressed the whole gang. He spoke sadly with a few tears sliding down his cheeks.

"This was a magical wish of mine. I had no idea how complicated of a wish it became or how it would turn out. I was so scared most of the time, but I had you as friends to cover for me and be there to protect me. I trusted you all every step of the way. Somehow, deep in my heart, I knew I would come out of this okay. I will miss you all so terribly much, and if it were a different time in life, then I would love to stay, but I can't. All I can take back is my memories of each one of you. Who knows? Maybe when I go forward to the future, you will all be there in a different life form. I just want you all to know that you will all be my best friends forever. I will never forget you." And with that, Matthew waved at them and said "Adieu," then he turned and walked away with Zerkin.

All six of his friends yelled "Adieu, Matthew, Adieu!" as Tiffany cried and Jacob held her in his arms to console her.

Zerkin and Matthew walked and talked a bit about what Matthew's life was like at home and what Zerkin would do since he was a full-blown wizard now. Then they reached the end of the meadows and just ahead was a forest dense with trees. The sun was shining brightly through the trees, which showed the path that Matthew was to take, and that's were they stopped.

"Matthew, this is whither ye must go. Matthew, grammarcy for lifting the fie. Thou art my best friend forever," Zerkin said as he hugged Matthew and dangled the red wristwatch that belonged to Matthew's mother in the air.

Matthew had a big grin on his face and accepted the watch back. "See, I could have stayed a bit longer and taught you all some really tight words."

They both laughed.

"Matthew, ye must remember, this silver arrow is sacred. It wilts connect thee to me. I am hence servant for the king and thee," Zerkin said proudly.

"Holy cow, I'm your master! This is going to be really hard not to tell my friends and family. If I say a word of what happened here, they will all think I'm nuts anyways."

"Ye canst dost as ye wishes."

"Fare thee well, my good friend," Zerkin said as he turned and walked away.

It was a real somber moment for Matthew. He felt like he was leaving his new family for good. He started on his trek back, not sure where he was going to end up. He thought, *I took a plane here and I'm walking back. That doesn't make much sense, but does any of this?*

Once again, the scenery was beautiful. The forest was rich in color, and he was drowning in the scent of pine in the air. It was so relaxing, and he felt really good. He was proud of himself. He felt like a man. As he should—he did an act that not many could have.

The birds were tweeting away. He could hear woodpeckers pecking away the bark from trees and squirrels jumping from branch to branch while they made their little chatter noises. Listening once again to the sounds of nature and the slight breeze in the air made him start to feel a little woozy.

Matthew quietly spoke to himself, "I think I can walk a little farther, and then I'll sit for a bit and just take a little nap. And then I'll continue on this path. I just feel so tired. Must be everything is catching up to me. Wow, I feel the same way I do after I take motion sickness pills."

He was able to walk another ten feet when he spotted a monstrous willow tree with branches touching the ground. He went under the branches and sat against the tree.

"This is the spot. I'll just close my eyes for a short bit and then regain my energy and head back home."

He closed his eyes and was asleep within seconds.

CHAPTER

20

"Okay, so its six thirty p.m. now. Dinner was ready a half hour ago. Matt was supposed to be back by six o'clock. Where do you suppose he is, Mark?" Sue questioned with an irritable tone.

"Looks like he let us down again huh," Mark replied.

"Well, I don't know what to think, maybe he injured himself and can't get back on time, I don't know but if he isn't back here in fifteen minutes we're going to look for him," Sue said.

Ben was running back to the campsite, from playing with his friends, when Sue yelled out to him, "Ben, did you see Matt come back yet?"

"No, Mom. See, I should have gone with him. Then I would have made sure that we got back on time," Ben said with a sneer.

"Well, I have to say, in truth, I agree with you Ben."

Sue went back to the picnic table and covered up dinner with lids and plastic wrap because she knew that they would have to go into the woods to find Matt. When she was done, she grabbed Ben's hand and walked over to Mark.

"Well, come on, dear. I think we had better go look for him. Thank goodness, it doesn't get dark until nine thirty," she said.

"Don't you think that Ben should stay here in case Matt does come back from another direction? If there is no one here, he'll think we abandoned him," Mark questioned.

"Ya, you're probably right. Will you be all right at the tent here, Ben, while we go search for your brother? We shouldn't be more than a half hour or so," Sue reassuringly asked.

"No problem. I'll ask one of the other boys if they want to play a game of cards." Ben was delighted because now no one was going to safeguard the snacks. "Hehehe," he laughed to himself as they walked off.

Sue looked back toward Ben and yelled, "And stay out of the snacks or you'll spoil your dinner!"

As normal, Ben pretended he didn't hear his mom.

Sue and Mark were on the trail to find Matthew. As they got deeper into the trail, they noticed bubblegum wrappers wedged between branches every couple of hundred feet.

"Looks like Matt is using his Boy Scout skills," Mark chuckled. "Well, we know he has some smarts," Sue replied.

They did enjoy their walk through the trail even though they had to hustle because it would be dusk shortly.

"This is a lovely spot, Mark. I would love to do this hike with you tomorrow. The aroma of the pine, the fresh air, and the beauty of the landscape is just incredible."

"I agree, we'll pack our lunch and take the hike just by ourselves."

They were following the trail for about forty-five minutes and were so engrossed in the beauty that they almost forgot why they were on the trail in the first place when Sue said, "This is bizarre. We should have found him by now. We should have passed him on this trail by now, don't you think?"

"Ya, I do. We had better start walking faster just in case he is farther out then we thought. I don't think he would have gone off the trail without putting a marker down," Mark said.

"Look at those stunning willow trees, Mark. They must be very very old. I wish I had my camera. I'll make sure to bring it tomorrow."

Then she spotted the plastic wrap from Matthew's sandwich on the ground.

"Well, look what I found. That litterbug, he left his sandwich wrap and banana peel on the ground," Sue said with frustration as she picked up the garbage.

"And his empty water bottle," Mark said, annoyed.

They continued to stride over to the enormously hefty willow trees and then they stopped.

They froze in disbelief. Directly in front of them was a shadowed outline of someone lying on the ground.

CHAPTER

21

"*Matthew!*" both Sue and Mark yelled with fear as they ran up to him lying on the ground under the willow tree.

There was Matthew sprawled out on the ground under the tree, lifeless to the world.

Mark lifted Matthew's head and Sue shook Matthew's arm. Slowly, Matthew opened his eyes and came alive again. The look in Matthew's eyes was like looking into a stranger. He had a confused look in his face.

"Give him a minute, Sue. Let him fully wake. We don't know if he is in shock or what may be the matter."

So they gave him some time, and Sue sat on the ground and put Matthew's head on her lap while Mark was holding his hand and trying to talk to him asking what had happened.

A few minutes went by when finally Matthew blinked several times and sat up and looked at both his mom and then his dad and said, "Dad, Mom? Am I really back?"

"Back from where Matthew?" Sue asked.

"From my journey. How long have I been gone for?"

"Well, if you mean did you make it back to the campground, then no. You must have fallen asleep. It's been about nine hours or so since you left the campsite, Matt," Sue said.

"Are you sure you didn't hurt yourself, Matt? You've been out here a long time," Mark asked.

Before Matthew opened his mouth to speak, he thought about what he would say to his parents, because they wouldn't believe what had happened. He would have to tell them over time to make it believable.

He thought to himself, there was no way he was only gone for nine hours. It must have been a couple of days. After all he went though? *No way!*

"Um. No, Dad, I didn't hurt myself. I just had the most fantastic journey through these trails, but I am glad you found me, because I am ready to go home."

"Home! Matthew, the weekend isn't over yet! Your mom and I want to do some hiking around here while you watch your brother, and that's our plan for tomorrow. So just for the record, we have yet another day before heading back to city," Mark explained.

"Sure, no problem," Matt said as they slowly helped lift him to his feet. "Do you guys believe in wishes or miracles or just strange happenings?" Matt asked.

"Well, miracles, yes. Strange happenings, yes. Wishes, sometimes. Why, Matt?" Mark asked guardedly.

"Well, I don't know. Something strange did happen to me out here this afternoon, and I just don't know what to think about it," Matt said as he was looking around the ground under the willow tree for his silver arrow, which was his proof.

"What are you looking for Matt?" Sue asked.

"I'm looking for something very special that was given to me by a friend." "You made a friend out here?" Mark asked.

Matt found it. It was lying under some leaves at the base of the tree trunk. He picked it up and examined it to make sure it made the journey back safely too. He turned to show his parents, who now had very surprised looks on their faces.

"Where did you ever get that?" Mark asked as he reached out for the silver arrow.

"It was given to me as a gift by someone very special. It's a long story, and I can't tell it in just a few minutes," Matt said as he looked nervously into his parents' eyes.

Mark was looking it over very carefully, turning it and reading the inscription on it.

1769
To my eldest heir Vincent. May this arrow be used to save lives
King Edward

"This is a very, very old arrow, Matt. I mean very old. This is an antique and could be worth a lot of money. Where did you get this?"

"I told you, it was given to me by a very special person. I had to do him a favor, and in return, he gave it to me." Matt was very nervous about telling his parents the story because he knew they wouldn't believe him and would think that he was (*a*) either sick, (*b*) hurt his head, or (*c*) concocting up this story.

"What favor?" Mark asked nervously.

Sue grabbed Marks hand and squeezed it tight, afraid of what Matt was going to say that he did for the arrow.

"Well, Mom and Dad, it's a long story, so why don't we just start heading back to camp, and I'll tell you on the way."

"Sure, sounds like a good idea since we are going to run out of daylight soon," Mark said.

"Well, it all started the first night we got here, remember? We were having dinner, and something bright flew in the sky. We first thought it was a shooting star, and then it looked like a dog. Remember?"

"Ya, we remember," both Mark and Sue said tensely.

"Well, anyways, the next day, I started out on my adventure, remember?"

"Yes."

"Okay, then, here is where it gets good. So I'm walking for a while, and I decide to sit under that huge willow tree you guys found me under. I start to get hungry, so I sat down and ate my lunch and snacks."

Mark pipes up. "Which, by the way, you left your garbage spewed all over the place here!"

"No, I didn't, Dad. I picked it all up. That was probably Zerkin."

"You had better continue on with the story."

"Okay, so I'm eating, and then I hear a noise in the bushes. Then it gets closer. It sounds like its rustling in the leaves. So I looked over my shoulder, and I see this dog. Well, I thought it was a dog. Anyways he had a long fuzzy tail and a stretched snout, and it was way too big for his face. He was probably medium size like forty-five pounds. His nostrils were awfully large, and you know he was kind of cute, but had a grumpy-looking mouth. His ears stood up straight and were pointed, and his eyes were yellow and they were bulging from his face. His claws were razor sharp and long. I mean he was freaky looking."

"Anyways, I gave him some of my lunch, and he loved it. He even did acrobatics for me. He jumped up in the air and did somersaults. Then he was playing games on me. He kept taking Mom's red watch."

Sue quickly interrupted. "Did you lose my watch, Matthew?"

"No, Mom, I have it here in my pocket." He reached for it and gave it back to her. "So he's playing these games and disappears on me. Next thing I know, he is like one hundred feet in front of me, further into the woods. So I go after him because I had to get Mom's watch back. Again he disappears, and I find him another one hundred feet in front of me. What he was trying to do was have me follow him. Well to make a long story short. I did, and when I got to where he took me, there was this beautiful, humongous castle across the river with a bridge that led to it. So I went over the bridge, and when I got there, there was a voice telling me to make a wish. I didn't believe it at first, but after a while I thought, "What the heck! What can it hurt?" So I did, I wished that I was living in the medieval period, but I also wanted to wish for a plane ride. I figured If I had a chance for a wish to come true, why not ask for two? Anyways, I walk through the humongous doors like it tells me to, and the next thing I know, I'm sitting on a plane!"

"Stop right there, Matt. This is starting to sound like a dream not reality!" Mark said.

"Are you sure you didn't hit your head or something, Matt?" Sue asked.

"No, Mom, and no, Dad. I knew you wouldn't believe me, and I knew you would think I hit my head or dreamt this, but it's all true. How can you explain this sword?" Matt said assertively.

Both Sue and Mark looked at each other with frowning eyes.

"Oh, also, I have something else to show you." He pulled his knapsack from his shoulder and opens it and digs around until he finds the silver dragon pendant that Rhymer Raymond dropped in the underground tunnel. He handed it to his father.

Mark examines it and said "This is also very old. You can tell by the color of the silver and the carvings on it" as he hands it back to Matthew.

"Okay, go on, Matt," Sue said.

"So anyways as I said I was on this plane. This part of my wish came true, so I knew I was going somewhere medieval. So this lady comes up to me. I guess she is the flight attendant, and she knows my name, but it's not my name. It's Sir Matthew, son of King Vincent and Queen Patricia," Matthew said with excitement.

"Okay, okay. Stop, Matthew!" Mark choked. "That's quite enough. This is a dream. It may seem like reality to you, but it is a dream. If you were on a plane, then where is the airport? You probably hit your head like your mom said and had a wonderful dream, but as you can see, you are here now. And as for the arrow, well, let's just chalk that up to finders keepers, losers weepers, okay?" Mark said.

Matthew knew he would get nowhere with his parents and decided to end the story there. Sometime and somehow, he would find someone to believe him. He had a big portion of the proof with him. All he had to do was try out the silver point on the arrow and see if Zerkin appeared. In time, when he felt it would be the right situation, he would give it a try. "Fine, but you guys don't know what you are missing."

"Why don't you write it up as a story for your essay when you get back to school. Who knows, it might be a hit with the kids." Sue said with a big smile on her face.

"It may even get you an A in English." Mark said with a smile.

So they made it back to camp, and Ben and his friends were sitting there at the picnic table, waiting for them. As Matt and his parents entered their campsite, Ben ran up to Matt and threw his arms around him, and Matt actually reciprocated.

"Good to see you, bud," Matt said.

"Really? You're happy to see me?" Ben asked.

"Sure! Why not? You're the only brother I have, and I wouldn't want you to turn on me!" Matt said sarcastically.

"Okay, guys. I'm going to warm up our dinner again, and we should be able to eat in about twenty minutes. *So no one leave this area!* " Sue demanded.

As she was warming up the dinner, Mark was gathering firewood for their campfire. Matt and Ben sat at the table, and Ben was curious as to what happened to Matt. He told him the same story that he told his parents, but went further and told him about Bianca and Zerkin, the wizard. Ben was mesmerized by his story but also would not believe him. Matt figured if anyone believed him it would be Ben. Then he showed him the silver- tipped arrow.

"That could belong to anyone, Matt. Maybe the person who this belongs to dropped it. Maybe he wants it back. Wouldn't you feel bad if he wants it back, Matt?" Ben questioned.

"If it makes you feel any better, I will let the camp host know that I have it, and if someone does claim it, they have to perfectly describe it before I would give it up." Knowing that no one could claim it because of where it came from, Matt was not worried at all.

"Okay, that's pretty good of you, Matt. Hey, Matt, after dinner, do you want to play a game with me?" Ben asked.

"Sure, buddy, I guess I can spend some time with you before we go home. It's only fair," Matt said.

"Are you sure you didn't hit your head? Maybe I should check for lumps or something," Ben asked.

"No, Ben. I'm fine."

Sue called everyone for dinner, where they sat quietly and ate. Surprisingly, no one said a word. Matt found it a little strange. He thought someone would bring up the majestic story that Matt had told them. But no. No one asked or said anything about it.

"Oh, Matt, remember that your dad and I are going to go on a hike tomorrow morning, so Ben is your responsibility, okay?" Sue said.

"No worries, Mom. You guys should do that trail walk. It's amazing, especially in the late morning or early day."

Matthew wanted to say "But watch out for the unusual doglike figures" but Zerkin was no longer a dog, and he doubted that the same thing would happen to his parents as it did him.

CHAPTER

22

The Journey home

It was early Monday morning. Mark and Sue wanted to get an early start on the trip home since it was an eight-hour drive back. So after breakfast, they started to take down the tents and pack up.

"Do we really have to go home today, Mom?" Ben asked.

"I'm afraid so, Ben. Three days, we said, and today is the day we go home, but if you really like this place, maybe we can bribe Dad into bringing us back before the summer is over."

"I'll start on him now, Mom!"

"Oh no, you won't. Just start packing up your stuff!" "Well, can I say good-bye to my friends first?"

"No, I know this game, Ben. We end up packing your belongings for you. You pack up first and then go say good-bye to your friends."

* * * *

They were done packing up the jeep.

"Matthew, can you go find your brother. We need to get going. We don't want to be driving in the dark," Sue said.

"Sure, Mom. I think he's at the lake, talking to Shaun and Lars." Matt ran over to Ben, and said, "Come on, kid. We're leaving now."

"Hey, Matt. I heard you got hurt in the forest? And you killed a witch and have a wizard as a friend?" Shaun said as he laughed uncontrollably.

Lars laughed with him.

Matt gave Ben a really snarly look, and Ben looked at Shaun and Lars and said, "I told you not to say anything!"

Matt grabbed Ben by the back of his shirt and dragged him to the jeep. "I'm sorry, Matt. I didn't think they would say anything to you."

"Well, I told you that in confidence. I can't trust you, Ben. That was something personal that happened to me!"

"Well, we're going home now anyways, and I won't tell anyone else what you said to me. I promise." Ben said.

"Whatever, just get in the jeep," Matt said angrily.

"Well, Matt," Mark said, "you never cease to amaze us. You did it again. Mind you, this year you didn't get the whole campground in an uproar, but you still caused a commotion among your family. If we could take your imagination and patent it, we would be rich."

They all laughed.

As they slowly approached the host office on their way out, Sue noticed a second man outside with the host.

"Oh, look, there's the hosts cousin. We met him the other day. Such a nice young man. Zak is his name, I believe."

Matt wasn't paying attention. He was searching through his knapsack for his iPod and headphones. When they reached the host office to say good-bye, the two hosts were standing outside to wish them farewell and wanted to be sure they had a good time.

When Zak looked into the back window to say good-bye to the boys, Zak looked straight at Matt and said, "Matthew, I hope you particularly had an epic time."

The voice was so familiar that Matt stopped searching in his knapsack and looked up. He immediately went tense, his jaw dropped open, and he was speechless. It was Zerkin.

He tried to speak, and Zerkin put his finger to his mouth, motioning Matthew not to say anything. He shook Matthew's hand, whispered something into his ear, and then winked at him. Then Mark slowly drove off.

Matthew was in shock trying to figure out how and why Zerkin was there. He turned around in his seat, looking out the back window and kept his eyes on Zerkin as they were driving away with a big smile on his face. Then he saw that yellow twinkle in Zerkin's eye. It was that magical twinkle, and it gave Matthew goose bumps on his neck. He knew he wasn't crazy—that journey was real, not a fantasy.

"Matthew, what was that all about with Zak? I didn't know that you had met him," Sue asked curiously. "He seemed to really like you. I mean, he didn't even shake your Dad's hand, just yours, and what did he whisper in your ear?"

"Oh ya, I met him the other day. We talked for a bit. He's a really nice guy. Oh, and earlier he was just showing me wooden statues he made and told me if I come back, he would show me how to make one," Matthew said with a smirk as he was still looking out the rear window.

What Zerkin really whispered into Matt's ear was that when he killed the witch and broke the spell, all the wooden gnomes in the forest turned back into humans again. So everyone in the village held Matt with the highest of respect. He thought Matt would like to hear that.

"So did everyone have a good time here at the Hidden Woods?" Mark asked.

"Ya, Dad, I had a terrific time, I met new friends, got more e-mail addresses, and just had a blast!" Ben wailed out.

"You know, Dad, I have to say that this was the best trip that I've ever been on, and I can't wait to come back," Matt said as he turned forward in his seat with the biggest smile on his face, put on his headphones, turned on his iPod and closed his eyes.

The End

Matt took his little brother, Ben, for granted. He believed that because Ben had a lot more growing up to do, was younger and smaller than him, he could treat Ben like his pet. So Matthew learned throughout his journey to respect his little brother. Going through his journey, he couldn't believe that his brother wanted him dead just to gain the power over the kingdom and its people. Taking that thought into real life, just maybe if he treated his brother with a little more courtesy and forgiveness, he would always have a brother that loves him.

He also learned that nothing is ever given to you for free. You have to earn it first. So during his journey, when things got tough and he couldn't take it anymore and wanted to wake up and be back home, he thought somehow Zerkin or someone could get him out of the situation that he was in. Little did he know that he had to work hard, believe in himself, go through a lot of misery and do things he thought he could never do just to get back to the safety of his home and family.

So if you work hard enough and believe in yourself, you will get to where you want to be in life.

We make our own destiny. If it's not in the stars to be something you are not, accept it, move on, and enjoy life. For we have but one life to live— make the most of it, and you will be happy.

So after this journey of Matt's, he learned to respect and not take for granted the people who were in his life whom he loved, for his family are the ones who truly filled his life with love and happiness.

ACKNOWLEDGMENTS

I have several people to thank in the making of this book.

- Bill Lasuta for his illustrations. Thank you for a speedy job on such short notice. You're a godsend!
- My husband, James Mennear, for building me a castle which gave me the inspiration to write this book. I have always loved fairy tales.
- Thank you to copyeditor Chris Anthony Ferrer, for your fantastic work in finding my errors.
- Several internet reference sites include *Life in Elizabethan England, Introduction to Middle Ages, Genealogy and Inheritance, Medieval England,* and *Dictionary of Medieval Words.*

Middle Age
Glossary of Words

abroad. In the open, at large

adieu. Good-bye

aghast. Terrified

airling. Airhead

alack. Darn it

Amiss. Not as things should be

anon. Later

apace. Quickly

art. Are

aught. Anything

bannock. Flat bread-cake

bebother. Bring extreme trouble upon

befallen. Happen, occur

benighted. Overtaken by darkness

beseech. Request or ask

beset. Assaulted by enemies

betimes. Very early in the morning

by my troth. I swear

by your leave. Excuse me or please

byre. Cow shed

canst. Can

carouse. Drink heavily

cesspool. Sewage

chide. Scold or nag

chine. Deep narrow ravine

cometh. Comes or coming

cosh. Hut, small cottage

couldst. Could

covert. A shelter

craven. Coward

daggle-tail. An untidy women

dank. Cold and damp

dost. Do

doth. Does

durst. Dare

e'em. Evening

encompass. Surround

enow. Enough

ere. Before

excellent well. Cool

fanger. A guardian, one who protects

fie. Curse

flesh-spades. Fingernails

forswear. Lie or cheat

fortnight. Period of two weeks

good den. Good afternoon or Good day

good morrow. Good morning

grammercy. Thank you

hark. Listen

haste. Hurry, rush

hath. Has

hazzah. Cheer

hence. From here on

hither. Here

honor. Constable or knight

how fare thee? How are you?

i bid you. I ask you

in truth. Really
leech. Healer, doctor
maidens. Young women of upstanding virtue
mayhap. Maybe, perhaps
methinks. I think
mischance. By accident
morrow. Tomorrow
muster. Collect, assemble
my goodman. My friend
n'er. (Pronounced "nair") never
naught. Nothing
nay. No
needest. Need
nigh. Near
none. Around 3:00 p.m.
oft. Often
outwit. Knowledge, information
outworn. Exhausted
over yonder. Over there
pallid. Pale
perchance. Perhaps
poppet. Young child
postern. A small rear door
prating. Babbling
pray pardon me. Excuse me
pray tell. Please tell
prithee. Please
privy. Restroom
saith. Said
sanctuary. Church, place to hide
shall/shalt. Will
spinney. Group of trees
spit-frog. Small silver sword
squiddle. To waste time with idle talk
stay. Wait or stop

swoon. Faint
teenful. Troublesome, irritating
thee/ye. You
thither. There
thou/thy/thine. Your / yours
thou art. You are
thou wast. You were
thou wert. You were
tidings. News
tis. it
tis most splendid. All right
tosspot. Drunk
ug. Fear or dread
vagabond. Homeless
verily. Very, truly
vespers. Around 6:00 p.m. or after dinner
what be your name? What's your name?
what say you. What did you say
whence. From where
wherefore. Why
whither. Where
wouldst. Would
widdershins. Unlucky, prone to misfortune
wilts. Will
wist. Knew, past tense
wit. To know
wondrous. Well, very well
worrit. Worry
wroth. Angry
wrought. Done or made
yammer. Wail, weep, whine
ye. You
yea/aye. Yes
yonder. Over there
yore. Long ago, years

www.ingramcontent.com/pod-product-compliance
Lightning Source LLC
Chambersburg PA
CBHW060751210726
48292CB00014B/2757